LIZ JENNINGS

Alone, Together

Short stories written during the

Covid-19 Lockdown period

LIONESS ::
WRITING LIMITED

Alone, Together

PUBLISHED BY LIONESS WRITING LTD 2020

Alone, Together was first published in Great Britain by
Lioness Writing Ltd in 2020

Liz Jennings can be contacted via her website at
Lizjenningswriter.com

ISBN: 1-9997464-9-X
ISBN-13: 978-1-9997464-9-0

Contents

PREFACE

THESE STORIES WERE WRITTEN in stolen moments, when my kids were sleeping in and my husband was engrossed in his own work and nobody required any snacks. I often felt like I was getting nothing much done during lockdown, so it's both surprising and encouraging to see that all those tiny patchwork pockets of writing time grew into this volume.

One of the pitfalls of writing stories is that friends who are kind enough to read them tend to assume they recognise either you or themselves. My previous collection left one dear friend convinced I'd done something dreadful in my back garden. I'd like to take this opportunity to say that none of the following characters are me, and neither are they based on friends or family. They feel real to me, because these characters have lived a while in my head. If they feel real to you, too, then that's wonderful. They're inspired by daydreaming, reading and listening to the news, pondering a million *What Ifs* and letting my imagination run free for a few unbothered minutes.

Sometimes someone will tell me a story and a detail will lodge in my mind and wait for its moment on the page. A friend of mine once told me a story about a funeral where everybody was very ill and had to keep running out of the chapel: this was the seed for the diarrhoea and vomiting detail in the crematorium in Blood and Taxidermy. But I must stress, my friend was at a very harmonious funeral for an adored relative. Writers are magpies, picking out the gems which sparkle to them and weaving them into nests of their own construction.

Some of the settings are based on real events: I did go on a boat party down the Thames just before lockdown, for my brother's 50th birthday. That trip was a useful setting for Jay to meet Isosceles. And the cemetery house and other landmarks described are loosely based on locations in and around Canterbury. I'm better at inventing people than places, so I let my characters roam around familiar locations, albeit with altered place-names, so that I can describe a scene without having to remember if I put a tree on the left or right of a building and so on.

For the wedding day, I owe a debt of thanks to Charles Dickens for inspiration, and to my neighbour, David, who lent me his cherished copy of Great Expectations. Miss Vashimah is, of course, an anagram of Miss Havisham, and I enjoyed playing with references to the story of the woman jilted on her wedding day. The story was inspired by hearing a phone-in on Radio 2, with brides speaking about how the Corona virus had ruined their plans for their big day. It was so sad, and I hope they all get the weddings they long for at some point. My bride, Miss Saltmarsh, only ever really saw her groom as an accessory, and is quite able to hold her wedding without him.

Lockdown provided an opportunity to imagine characters reacting to new problems, and I have loved exploring a few of them as they occurred to me. We are not back to 'normal' by any means as I write this, and I'm sure there will be many, many more stories written. Indeed, I suspect these weeks where we've been alone, together will continue to inspire new stories for years to come.

There were stories I felt I *ought* to write during this time, and stories I tried so hard to write, but that wouldn't come. At some point one needs to let go and say, this little offering - small as it is, limited as it is, lacking as it is - is mine: I have done my best with the characters and situations that came to me, and my hope now is that you might enjoy them.

With thanks,

Liz Jennings

Canterbury, July 2020

ISOSCELES

IT WAS ON A BOAT PARTY on the Thames that I met the man who was to change the course of my life.

I was introduced to him by Jack's wife. Jack was a friend of my fiancé, Tom. I'd never met Jack before, but, keen to prove something or other, I'd spent several hours earlier that week trawling the high street to choose a birthday gift and card for him. I'd wrapped the present while Tom signed the card: *Just like an old married couple*, I'd said.

Jack was thirty and his wife (whose name I don't think I was ever told) had organised the party for him. We were travelling on an old steamer, decorated with helium-filled balloons and bunting, from Kingston Bridge to Hampton Court via Teddington Lock, and back again.

The boat was heaving with all the friends, colleagues and relatives Jack's wife had been able to get hold of. The champagne was flowing. Cool young men and women dressed all in black were weaving between guests with silver trays laden with miniature treats of all kinds. The music was full-on 1990s to mark the decade of his birth, and was being ferociously chewed up by nostalgic twenty-somethings who dipped and lurched around the crowded room, grabbing each other and laughing at shared memories to each tune. They were watched with fond indulgence by the older guests – mostly relatives, these - who ferociously chewed up the hors d'oeuvres and danced their own verbal variations around one another with idle conversation. The crowd were as friendly as any you could wish to meet.

I stood at the edge, by the stairwell that led below-deck, and watched my fiancé catching up with old friends. We'd been engaged for six months. I watched Tom making his work friends laugh and I thought how handsome he looked, and saw how funny he must be being. I felt my path was set, and then I felt a touch on my arm.

"This is Isosceles," Jack's wife said, playing her part as the perfect hostess and making sure I had someone to stand with. He was tall, lean and broad, with greying blond hair that hung to his shoulders and a close cut beard that looked like it would give you sore skin were you to spend the evening necking with him. My thought made me blush, and I instinctively looked over at Tom, still laughing with his friends.

The man before me wore a Nehru jacket in a midnight blue-black, which set off his keen blue eyes perfectly. "Isosceles," Jack's wife held her palm towards me, "Meet Jay. Jay, meet Isosceles." Job done, she smiled her full-stop and disappeared into the noisy crush of bodies.

"Sorry," I said, raising my voice above the chatter around us and reaching out to shake his hand. "Did she say *Isosceles*?" I frowned and smiled all at once in a way I hoped was friendly, rather than mocking. I had heard his name perfectly clearly, but I knew that the only way I was likely to hold this man's attention was to keep asking questions about him.

"I was conceived in the '60s, what can I say?" He shrugged as if this was explanation enough.

"Are you named after the triangle?" I said, unable to supress a giggle. He smiled kindly, holding his own laughter in a closed mouth, watching me, to my great surprise, with what seemed to be genuine delight.

"There's a sentence you never thought you'd say today," he finally said, which kept me smiling. I raised my glass and so did he, and we toasted. "To mad old '60s names," he said.

"To mad old '60s names." We drained our flutes. A beautiful young man, his tan glowing burnt orange against his black shirt, came past with a tray of more champagne, and Isosceles took the empty glass from my hand, set both our glasses onto the tray and lifted two fresh ones for us in a movement so smooth that the waiter never even felt it happen as he glided past. "Thanks," I sipped again. "So, were your parents mathematicians?"

"Nothing so noble, I'm afraid." He paused, looked up at the roof and cleared his throat. I took his cue and waited for the punchline. "My mother had two chaps on the go at the same time, and she didn't know which of them was my father."

I clasped my lips as the laugh came. Champagne that had been in my mouth was forced up some mysterious inner working and was now halfway down my nostrils in a painful backfire and I began to cough. Rather than slap my back, or wait to see how it worked out, Isosceles hugged me to him warmly, wrapping his arm around my shoulder and sipping champagne so that his lips were by my ear. I felt the lightest brush of stubble through my hair.

"I've got a hanky in here somewhere," his other hand rifled through his jacket pockets. "Come on, you lovely woman," he said, dabbing at my face with his handkerchief, "Let's go out on deck."

I followed him in astonishment, I think I may even have had my mouth wide open with the shock of his words. I am, frankly, plain. My hair is dull brown, my eyes are a pale, cold blue, my skin is freckled (but not in a charming way), my figure is on the heavy side and my dress sense has never impressed a living soul. No one has ever called me 'lovely', and I don't expect anyone ever shall, unless they're making fun of me. But it didn't feel as if Isosceles was making fun of me.

The sky outside was grey, but the air was warm, and thick with the smoke of all the cigarettes that were being greedily sucked on out there. Tiny cottages nestled between vast glass fronted homes like mismatched beads on the sparkling necklace of the riverbank. Each house had its own mooring, some with dinghies and rowing boats, others with yachts. Each residence seemed to me equally desirable and each made me curious as to the people who had ended up in this enviable situation.

"Are you here with anyone?" Isosceles asked.

"My fiancé," I said, and looked back through the door to the dance floor where Tom had been. He wasn't there for me to point out now. "He's somewhere in here," I said, waving my hand generally at the boat. "It's his friend's birthday. I don't know anyone, really. He's terribly sociable and good at parties. I expect he's dancing somewhere." I sipped my champagne and stared across the water at Eel Pie Island, which sounded quainter than it looked, but was intriguing nonetheless. "I once went on a training course there," I said, holding my champagne flute towards the island. "I can't remember what for. I just remember being terribly excited about actually going onto an island with work, and then being rather disappointed that it didn't feel more... islandy."

"What do you do, workwise?" Isosceles lent an elbow on the rail and turned away from the view, so that he focussed on me. The directness of his gaze was hard to meet.

"I'm a trainee solicitor. To be honest, I'm a glorified administrator at the moment. But it's all part of the slog. I just need to keep going, and I'll get there in the end."

"Where's 'there', exactly?" he said, waving his glass at the word. I checked his face for criticism, but he seemed to be genuinely interested. Surely I wouldn't hold his attention much longer: I made my answer as short as possible.

"Oh, you know, a proper, grown-up solicitor. A house somewhere near Richmond Park with a flat by the sea for weekends. That's the dream."

"Richmond Park is lovely," he said.

"Yes, I could roam in there for hours," I smiled.

"What about your fiancé?"

"Oh, he's training to be an architect. He's almost there now. Another steady slog. He's just had an interview at Maugham Associates. Have you heard of them? They did The Mouse up in town. Very prestigious."

"Impressive," he said.

"They've won all sorts of awards," I said, then smiled. "Architects love awards. Tom's father is an architect, too. Hopefully Tom will win something, one day."

He smiled. Still, I waited for him to make an excuse and leave me, but he didn't.

"Jay is a very unusual name," he said. "Are you named after the bird?"

"Nothing so noble. I'm actually called Jayne, but... I don't know. Can I tell you something I haven't told anyone else?" The champagne and the desire to keep him with me were making me feel daring.

"You don't have to," he said. "But I'd love it if you did."

I felt the warmth flooding my cheeks and looked down at my drink. "Well, I want to. You see, I have always been so... so boring, I suppose. Yes, I'm boring. And to cap it all, I'm called Jayne, which is a pretty boring name. At school they called me Plain Jayne, of course, and also Boring Fat Jayne, which doesn't rhyme and is frankly, bloody hurtful."

"That is bloody, bloody hurtful," he said. As I watched him, his eyes filled with tears. They actually did, I kid you not. "God, *school!*" he said, with feeling.

"So when I got to university I told everyone my name was Jay. It didn't seem to rhyme with anything too onerous, and it is somehow completely different to Jayne."

"You're right, it is."

"Well it's alright for you," I said. "You have the most interesting name of probably anyone on this entire boat."

"It's quite as possible to have an interesting name and be a dull bugger as it is to have a dull name and be a glorious wonder," he smiled. "I like you."

What an out of place thing to say to a person! I mean, does anybody ever say that to you? Nobody has ever said that to me. The effect of his words was physical: they fell upon me like popping candy and treacle all at once. My eyes widened and probably bulged unattractively, and I became quite coquettish for a moment, then took a deep breath and met his eyes again and blew out a loud raspberry. "Well, I like you, too, Isosceles," I said, feeling full to the brim with that peculiar and gloriously English awkwardness.

And then the silence fell between us. I could think of nothing to say next, and he stood there smiling, and the pause lingered on like an overdue baby.

"Do you need to go?" I finally blurted out, unable to labour on in silence any longer.

"Nope," he smiled. "You?"

"Oh, no, no," I said.

"Will your fiancé be looking for you?"

"I don't expect so," I said, imagining Tom in his element, making connections.

"What's he like, your young man? Is he? Young?"

"Same age as me, twenty-nine."

"A wonderful age."

"Is it?" I said. "What makes you say that?"

"You're not finding it so?"

"So far, twenty-nine has been dreadful. Everyone expects me to be a grown-up and make proper, serious decisions. My Mother keeps on at me about getting on with having children and my Father says I should have made solicitor by now and can't understand that it's a slow process. And my brother is flying high as some sort of accountant, I don't understand his job, but he's running his own firm already and has the most enormous house, and I'm still renting and living with Tom, and I know Tom thinks I should be more ambitious. But I feel as if the need to make all these decisions is being forced upon me, and personally I'd rather never make a decision in all my life." I hiccupped, which rather emphasised my point, I felt. "Sorry, it must be the champagne speaking."

"It sounds like *you*, speaking," he smiled so kindly that I couldn't help it, I reached out and touched his beard.

"I just wanted to feel it," I said, blushing hotly.

"So, feel it," he said. "Feeling things is good." He laughed suddenly. "Sorry, that sounded like a dirty old man thing to say, like my next line would be, *You can feel this, if you like!*" We laughed.

"I'm sorry," I said. "I've embarrassed you."

"Not at all," he said. "I'm perfectly capable of embarrassing myself."

"I'm not used to talking for so long," I said.

"You feel you need to work to keep my attention?" He said.

I felt stripped bare for a moment. "Well, that's how it goes, isn't it? If you're not beautiful or interesting, you have to work at these things." I sniffed. "Now I sound full of self-pity. Unbearable. Sorry."

"I hope Tom makes you feel as wonderful as I suspect you are, Jay," he said.

"Tom?" I looked intently into those bright blue eyes.

"That's what husbands and wives are meant to do for one another, isn't it. We're here to make each other feel as wonderful as we are. Maybe more so."

I stared, mouth hanging open again, without a word in my head. Finally, I pulled myself together. "What about you?" I asked. "I haven't even asked what you do, I'm sorry, that's so rude of me."

"Not at all," he shook his head. "I've been having a great time getting slowly sozzled with you, Jay. And, in answer to your question, I do all sorts of stuff."

"That sounds like you're either in investments or drugs," I said, taking a swig that emptied my glass. "Please tell me it's drugs."

He laughed. "Not drugs. That's something I've never done."

"I thought everyone did drugs in the '60s," I said.

"Well, I was only five years old when the '60s ended, so that would have been going some." He drained his glass, too, and then performed the same depositing and lifting manoeuvre as a young woman with unnaturally red hair came past with a tray of more drinks. "Nah, I just never saw the attraction of following a set path in life. I don't know, it's like, you're born and then you're put into an education system that gets you trying all sorts of new things, while simultaneously whispering, conform, conform, conform," he said.

"I'm not with you," I tilted my head.

"Well, it's like they say, *You're good at maths – you should be an accountant!* Or *You're good at dance – work harder at your maths!*"

"That's so true!" I said. "I loved art at school. And I was good at it. But all the way through you're told, you'll never make a living at this. Keep it as a hobby. Get a proper job."

"Yes. That's it. And, perhaps it's because of the times I grew up in, or the family I grew up in, but I just didn't see any attraction in following those rules."

"So what did you do?"

"Oh, I've done all sorts of things. And I'm still discovering." He shifted his weight and held his hands out. "Life is pretty wonderful, you know. And I hear myself and I know I must sound like a daft old man to you. But there's so much to see and do! And now I sound like a kids TV presenter. But I can't help it! The world is wide and vast, and it's full of the most wonderful people. People to meet and love, and be loved by."

"I love you," I said, hearing myself and wishing I were dead. "That's the champagne speaking," I murmured.

"But I love you too," he said. "This is the way it should be. You meet people, and you just love who they are. Not sex. No, I'm not hugely bothered by sex, to be honest. I've made a mess of things whenever I've involved sex. But just… there's something very pure about looking to love the people we meet. There's something utterly open and thrilling about it. I'm so thrilled to have met you."

I began to cry.

"Aww, there you go," he smiled and wrapped me in a tight embrace. "Take my hankie. You clearly need a hanky more than me, today."

"It's just that… you're life sounds so beautiful… so free."

"Well, I have to pay some bills. But yes, it is pretty great. You can do it, too."

"Me? No."

"Sure. Listen, I've just come from New Zealand, where I've been helping tour guides on a glacier. Every day I got to walk across this insane ice block landscape, hopping over little streams and cutting steps into the blue-white mountain beneath me. It was incredible. And the guy I was working with was like a bear. I mean, he looked like a bear, he was huge, his hands were like paws. He was terrific, a beautiful person. He made the most incredible chicken soup, and his wife was this tiny, tiny, fairy-like woman who bred angora rabbits in their backyard. She was wonderful."

"They sound great," I smiled, already bored by his story. I hate hearing people's travel stories.

He laughed suddenly. "You have the glazed look of someone listening to a tedious travel story," he said.

I was furious with myself. "I'm so sorry," I said, "I didn't mean to."

"It's ok, I'd be the same. Travel stories are pretty dull."

"Well, they're not. Of course they're not. You had an incredible time. You had an amazing experience. It's just... I don't know. I think they're like listening when your partner wakes up and tells you their dream in great detail. It sort of only means something to you if you're *in* it, you know? It's not that you don't care, it's just that you're not *in* it, and you just can't understand it somehow, it doesn't make sense to you."

"Yes," he said. "Or like looking at other people's photographs of events you weren't at and don't know anyone at. I hate listening to people's dreams, unless I'm in them, and then I absolutely *have* to know every detail."

"That's it exactly," I said. "So, where did you go after New Zealand?"

"Well, I had a very brief stopover in China, but literally a couple of days, and then I came back here. I've got a job lined up in Whitby, working at the abbey up there. It's a place I've always wanted to spend some time in, so that's what I'm doing next."

"Everything I've ever done has been so focussed on career development," I said.

"Well, what else would you like to develop?" he asked. I was taken aback by the question.

"I'd like to get back into my art," I said.

"Is there a way you could live your life so that you got to do that?" he asked.

"I like cooking, too. I've always secretly wanted to work in a sandwich bar, making sandwich fillings. And soups. I'd like to make soups for a café."

"Well, that job does exist. All over the world."

"And I'd like to learn to grow flowers," I said.

"Have you seen the tulip fields of Holland?"

"Never. Well, on a postcard in my Mum's kitchen, once. It was lovely."

"I worked there one spring. Holland is a terrific country, full of people with a brilliant sense of humour. Very close to English humour, actually, but I won't bore you with my travel stories."

I smirked. "I do love you," I said, the words coming easily now. "But, listen," I straightened up suddenly, "You just said you were in China?"

"I was. Just for a week. A bit of a mini-break on my way here."

"Did you see anything of this virus they keep talking about on the news?"

"The Corona thing? I think I did a bit. They weren't really reporting on it over there, but there were certainly a lot of face masks being worn."

"I heard it started at a market there," I said, feeling suddenly more sober.

"Yes, and I can see how that could happen. I spent quite a lot of time wandering around various markets, and the way they butcher animals in the open air is something I haven't yet seen anything like, elsewhere."

"Did you go to Wuhan?"

"Actually I did. I mean, it was all still very busy. People were going about their daily business, getting on with life."

"But you feel ok?"

"Oh, yes, I'm fine. Hopefully this whole thing will be contained, although with all the flights in and out of China it's hard to see how they could do that."

"I heard there had been a few cases in Italy already."

"Let's hope it's kept to a minimum. But, listen, enough of this gloom. I'd love to meet your fiancé," he said.

And, as if he'd been summoned, Tom appeared. He was with four other young men who looked identical to him in their skinny jeans and checked shirts. He glanced over at me and I saw a look pass across his face, the merest shadow of a frown, and I knew that he was not pleased to see I had been leaning over the arm rail of a boat, sharing champagne with an insanely handsome stranger. Suddenly I wasn't keen to introduce him to Isosceles.

"That's him, there," I said, my voice a bit flat to my drunken ears.

"Does he treat you well?" Isosceles studied Tom, and I watched Isosceles studying Tom.

"He works very hard," I said, realising that I hadn't matched the right answer to the question but unable to think of any other response. "He'll go a long way. Everyone says."

Isosceles turned to me. "Well, I wish you all the joy in the world, Jay." He leaned over and planted a kiss on my forehead. I watched Tom out of the corner of my eye, but he continued talking with his friends.

The boat came in to dock. The party was over.

"I can't believe we spent the whole time together," I said, mouth wide open in a big, silly smile at Isosceles.

"It's been wonderful," he said. "I'm so glad I met you." We hugged, and parted, and he disappeared into the shopping crowds of Kingston. My arm was gripped from behind with a firmness that I recognised as Tom's, and we made our own way back to the train station. All the way back to Clapham, Tom interrogated me about my new friend, and accused me of making a fool of him with my brazen flirting, and reminded me how no one else would look at me with anything other than pity and that I should pull myself together, how disgusting I was to be drunk in public, and what would I do if someone from that party came to my office for professional help and recognised their solicitor as the drunken slag from the boat they'd been on last week? I was sick on the train, and Tom was so disgusted by me that he went in to the next carriage so that he didn't have to look at me.

When I got home, I was sick again and went straight to bed. Tom didn't talk to me for the rest of the weekend, but I felt his disappointment in every corner of the flat, and in every stiff move he made. I couldn't escape my shame.

It was three days later that I began to cough. Just in fits that lasted about an hour, at first. I couldn't stop. It was a hard, dry cough that hurt my throat. My temperature rose steadily until it reached fever point. My lungs seemed to be filling up with straw. It was Mother who persuaded Tom to take me into hospital, where I am, now.

No one's allowed to visit. Yesterday, Tom sent me a note. In it, he told me that the bloke I'd been throwing myself at (his words) had died. He'd got the virus, and I'd caught it through my embarrassing behaviour (his words again). Isosceles had also had the beginnings of prostate cancer, which he hadn't known about. Now he was gone.

I sat in my bed, my breathing laboured through the oxygen mask I was wearing, and wept a little. The mucus made by the crying made it impossible to breathe properly at all, so I tried to go through the experience of crying without shedding any tears. It didn't seem real. I needed to picture Isosceles striding through the grounds of Whitby Abbey, loving every tourist he met.

My Mother wrote me letters, several a day, full of love and begging me to heal, as if I had any say in the matter. She passed them to nurses, who brought them to me. The nurses looked like angels from my fetid, grimy sheets. They gave themselves without question, and kept me alive.

One day, one of them said, "You're improving. You're going to make it, Jay."

I managed to pull the faintest echo of a smile for her. "When I do," I said, "I know exactly what I'm going to do first."

Blood and Taxidermy

THE LAST TIME I'D SEEN AUNTIE MARGARET had been over a decade ago at Uncle Derek's funeral. I was fourteen at the time. It had been a memorable service for three reasons: firstly, there had been a diarrhoea and vomiting bug doing the rounds and at least half the small congregation had it. There was a constant urgent coming and going as people ran out of the chapel at the crematorium to go to the toilet. Most people never made it that far. I will always remember coming out of the service to the sight of luminous yellow splatters of vomit on flowerbeds and lumpish vomit running down brown brick walls, and I shall never forget the smell that hit my nostrils like English mustard.

Secondly, the celebrant passed out when he got up to speak and had to be relieved by my mother waving her order of service over him and slap-slap-slapping his pale face until he came round.

Thirdly, Uncle Derek had been conducting an extra-marital affair for the last fifteen years of his fifty year marriage. Auntie Margaret had known, but had kept it between the three of them. However, Phyllis, Uncle Derek's lover (the thought of that makes me queasy) came to the funeral and sat in the front row, across from Auntie

Margaret and, much to my teenage delight, Auntie Margaret had leaned forward, made eye-contact with Phyllis and hissed at her. Actually hissed. Like a furious cat.

I didn't want to check in on her once a week during lockdown, or take her groceries for two reasons: firstly, I didn't want to go to the supermarket any more than was strictly necessary because I was terrified by the idea of getting the virus. And when I say terrified, I mean *terrified*. Every day I seemed to acquire some strange symptom out of the blue, but none of them ever really developed. They came in the form of a sudden hot flush to my face, or stabbing pains across my body, a scratchy throat or a succession of shocking sneezes. Then, as soon as they'd given me a good scare, they would disappear like smoke on the wind.

Secondly, I was afraid of Auntie Margaret. What if she hissed at *me*?

However, I had to check on her whether I liked it or not for one reason and one reason only: Mother told me to. "She's family," Mother said. "That's all the reason you need, you selfish boy."

Already reluctant, once the plan rolled out, I came to dread my Friday delivery for three new reasons: firstly, Auntie Margaret's bungalow was ugly. I don't just mean it was bland or boring, I mean it was aesthetically vomit-inducing. In decades past, sometime around the point when fashion replaced style, Uncle Derek had extended the bungalow on both sides in several stages, doing all the work himself using materials stolen from whatever building site he was managing at the time. Throughout the

1980s he had regularly filled the back of his horrid white van with bricks and cladding of all the worst sorts. The central, original section of the bungalow was a rank brown brick. On the right (in what Uncle Derek called the East Wing), light pink bricks completed a small window-less section, then a pebble-dashed end completed the look (which was no look at all. If that look had a name, it might be called The Horrible Look.) On the left (known as the West Wing, without a hint of irony), yellow bricks sat, badly laid with randomly thick and thin mortar (Uncle Derek was training a new labourer and had made him practice on the bungalow at weekends). This side was completed with a panel of fake stone cladding and a rounded turret made of breeze blocks which never got plastered but remained naked grey with mortar oozing between each block like mustard from a tower of poisonous burgers. To call it an offence to the eye is to understate. It was like a Disney castle reimagined by a psychopath.

Secondly, Auntie Margaret scared me. She was highly prone to saying things that embarrassed me, or made me worry.

Thirdly, there was nowhere for me to sit, and it became immediately clear that Auntie Margaret expected me to stay and talk. Actually, she expected me to stay and listen. Yes, *that's* a more accurate recording of the situation.

But Mother said there were two good reasons why it had to be me: firstly, my sister had her own family to look after and couldn't be expected to do more than that because that was bad enough. Secondly I was a selfish man who, like all men before me, had never thought of another living soul in my life and it was time I learned.

The first time I came, I approached the horrible bungalow with caution, afraid that the very thorns on the nasty roses that lined the disgusting crazy paved path (made with, no doubt, stolen crazy paving), could be carrying the deadly disease.

I placed the bag of shopping by the front door, which was irritatingly off-centre, and had been painted diarrhoea brown.

I knocked on the door and ran back down the path to stand by the gate that Uncle Derek had stolen from another of his sites.

She didn't answer the door.

I waited… and waited… and waited… She obviously wasn't coming.

I ran back to the door and just as I was about to knock, literally with my hand on the stolen horse-shoe knocker, she appeared behind the frosted glass. I saw the heavy curtain pull back and she opened the door. My feet ignored my command to run and I stood with my hand where the knocker had so recently been, face to face with my dreaded Auntie. She stood, scowling at me, her pink head poking out of the slit in the top of a mustard kaftan, her orange hair set high, her lips and teeth smeared with the same waxy peach lip-stuff.

"What are you doing so close?" she said, flicking the backs of her hands at me. "Get back! Get back!"

I turned and ran down the path to the gate.

"You can stay there," she said. "Stay so that I can check you've done this right." And she unpacked the contents of the shopping right there, wiping each item with a bleach-soaked jay-cloth while I twitched with fear.

She said the name of each item as she cleaned it, as if she were teaching me new words. Never mind the fact that I'd been the one who'd found it all on the shelves in the first place.

"Tinned mackerel in tomato sauce. Yes," she said, holding it toward me, wiping it down and then placing it on the front door step. "Tinned rice pudding. Yes." She placed it down. "Tinned custard. Yes." Down it went. "Tinned prunes. Yes."

"Well that's alright, then," I said, backing away, but she held her jay-cloth up at me.

"I'm talking," she said.

"I thought you were just listing," I said.

"What's the difference?"

I tried to think what the difference was.

"You should stay there for three reasons," she said. "Firstly, you might have forgotten something. Secondly, you probably got something wrong. Thirdly, I might need to send you to get something else."

She was right, of course.

"Your Mother always said you were selfish," she said.

I felt the tears springing hotly to my eyes, so I turned and ran back to my car. Behind me, I heard her shout. *"SUCH A BABY!"*

My Mother telephoned me later that day.

"What did you do to upset your Auntie Margaret so badly?" she asked.

"I don't know. Nothing." I said. I'd been biting my nails all afternoon and my fingertips were sore.

The following Friday, I approached what I was now secretly calling The Bungalow of Terror with another bag of shopping.

This time, I knocked good and hard, before sprinting down the path to the stolen gate.

When she opened the door, I noticed three things: firstly, despite her hair being sprayed solid in an upward style, a line of grey was taking ground from the roots up. Secondly, the brown kaftan she wore today made her look like a crazy nun dressing as a monk. Thirdly, her lime green crocs didn't go with her outfit at all.

"Stay there, you," she said, reaching for the contents of the bag, jay-cloth at the ready. "Don't you go until I say you can."

I waited.

"Don't you go," she said.

"I'm not going anywhere," I said.

"Good. Don't."

She pulled a Pot Noodle from the bag and wiped it down.

"Chicken and mushroom," she said, "Yes."

There was no normal answer to that. I stood there, watching her in the midst of the crime scene that was her home, and I wished my sister had never got married or had children. Then I saw something small, furry and unidentifiable in Auntie Margaret's West Wing window.

"What's that?" I pointed. Without looking up from wiping down her third Pot Noodle, she said, "That's Lancelot."

"Lancelot?"

"He's a mole."

I squinted hard, but I could not make Lancelot into any kind of recognisable mole. His hands seemed to be on backwards and he appeared to have mint imperials for eyes.

"A mole?"

"Chicken and mushroom. Yes," she said, then, "Your Uncle Derek had a brief foray into the world of taxidermy."

"He did that himself?"

"Dairy Lee Triangles. Yes, he did."

"Why have you put it there?"

"Long life milk. Yes. Because little children are going around looking for teddy bears. Haven't you got one in your window?"

"I live on the seventh floor," I said.

"You don't think children look up?" she said. "Alright. You can go."

The next week, there was a new creature in the West Wing window.

"Is it a cat?"

"Not just any cat, you idiot." Auntie Margaret said. I flinched and she saw it. "Ah, come on," she said. "Don't tell me you never got called an idiot before. That I won't believe. Not of you."

I stood my ground. I did want to turn and run. But I stood my ground for two reasons. Firstly, I wanted to know about the cat. Secondly, I had come out in my slippers by mistake and there were impossible to run in.

"Tell me about the cat, then," I said.

"Tinned mackerel in tomato sauce. Yes." She said, then, "His name was Bonaparte, and he was the best cat on this road. He could beat any of the other cats in a showdown, and the dogs, too. People would bring their dogs from across town to see if Bonaparte really was as great as they'd heard. And he was. Beat 'em all. Every single one."

"He sounds scary."

"He was scary. That was the whole point."

"How is that the point of a cat?"

"We never even stroked him until he died."

"I just think that's sad."

"We respected him too much to patronise him. Stroking patronises a cat."

"Why are his arms out so wide? Why is he so… flat?"

"He got run over."

"Out in the road here?" I looked down the quiet cul de sac. "That would have been very bad luck."

"Your uncle reversed over him."

"Oh." That explained the flatness. "Do the children *like* seeing him?"

"You bet they do! They *love* him! Everybody loved Bonaparte. And now the legend lives on! Chicken and mushroom. Yes."

"I'd better go," I took a step backwards.

"Got something you have to rush off for, do you? Busy, are you? Just you, everybody else with nothing to do, except for you?"

I turned and left.

"How could you leave her so soon?" My mother said over the telephone that evening. "You're the only human contact she has."

I could think of five reasons, but I didn't bother sharing any of them with Mother. There was no point because as soon as I'd thought of them, I immediately thought of three reasons why telling Mother would be a bad idea.

The next Friday, Auntie Margaret was waiting for me.

"You're late," she said.

"Am I?"

"What can possibly have kept you?"

"I don't know."

"It's not like you've got anyone else to think about."

"Stand back while I put your bag down," I said.

"I haven't got the lurgy," she said, standing her ground.

"But *I* might have," I said.

"Oh!" This took her by surprise, which was very satisfying. She pulled her purple kaftan tightly around her and stepped backwards into the Bungalow of Terror. I took hold of my advantage while I had it.

"Your hair looks stripy now."

She touched her hairline where the grey was steadily advancing, but said nothing. It didn't feel as good as I'd imagined it would feel when I'd rehearsed saying it last night. I put the bag down and glanced over at the front window to see what hideous deformed creature lurked there this week to thrill the kiddies.

"Is that a badger?" The dark grey-brown, black and white mangled heap seemed to have three limbs coming from its right shoulder.

"Roadkill."

"Killed by Uncle Derek?"

"My, but you're in a spiteful mood today," she said. "You get that from your Father's side."

I turned and left.

"I haven't checked my shopping." I heard her call after me. And, then, "*Selfish!*"

When Mother called that evening I gave her three reasons why I never wanted to see Auntie Margaret ever again. She, in turn, gave me one reason why I had to keep going. "She's family," she said.

What could I say to that? There's no answer to it.

The next Friday, I was early. I knocked hard, put the bag down and retreated to the safety of the gate.

A roundly inflated, shiny puffer fish hung from a string in the window to delight the neighbourhood's toddlers.

Auntie Margaret opened the door. She was back in the mustard kaftan. She patted her greying hair, which was not up this week, but hanging limply over her shoulders. She reached down for the bag.

"Thank you," she said, without meeting my eye. She took the shopping inside and closed the door.

I stood and waited, but she did not reappear. I waited some more, but nothing changed.

As I turned to leave, a family out for their daily stroll approached. Their two young children were skipping along and racing towards the Bungalow of Terror. The third was being pushed in a pram by a skinny woman with stringy hair and hot pink claws for nails.

"Mummy, it's a fishy! It's a fishy!" The children hopped and squealed.

The parents stopped – too close for my liking. I stepped back.

"They're brilliant, aren't they?" The father indicated my Auntie's weird window display.

"Um," was the singular response that came to mind.

"We come most days to see what monstrosities the old bag's stuck up in the window. Keeps the kids entertained."

I looked from him to his wife, to the baby in the pram she pushed, to his two hopping daughters.

"Mind you, I remember that evil cat of hers from when I was a kid," the man went on. "Used to terrorise the neighbourhood, it did. And her husband was a right git. You know, this whole house is basically made of knocked off stuff, yeah? He built it himself with materials he nicked from the building sites he worked on. Oh, yeah! He even used to rope in free labour from the kids on the YTS schemes."

I looked at the house. I definitely saw the thick curtain behind the front door move.

"Her husband was carrying on for years and years with a woman from down the other end of the road," he said, jabbing his thumb over his shoulder to indicate where the other end of the road was. "She still lives there to this day. Ooh, the cat fights those women had over that bloke, and him a total git!"

"Alright, that's quite enough," I said. The man looked surprised, as did I.

"It's only what everyone round here says," he said. "It's all true. Nothing wrong with saying what's true."

I saw the net curtain twitch behind the blowfish.

I looked at the Bungalow of Terror, taking it all in. Auntie Margaret had not yet offered to pay me for a single grocery delivery. She had phoned my mother repeatedly to complain about me and she found fault with everything I did. She never made me feel anything but small. She'd called me pathetic and selfish. It was pretty clear how she felt about me. Well, I felt the same way.

I turned to the man, who was now taking pictures of the blowfish on his mobile phone, a superior, mocking look on his face.

"Everything you've said is all highly offensive to me for three reasons," I said. "Firstly, the house is different, but it would be a very boring world if everybody and everything were exactly alike, wouldn't it? Secondly, her husband was not kind to her. All the more reason for you to show kindness, now. And, thirdly, I agree, the window decorations are on the unusual side, but I can see clearly how they are keeping you entertained, so I don't comprehend why for a moment you would wish to complain about those."

I could see Auntie Margaret now, holding the curtain back and watching me, and looking at the rude family.

"Sorry, mate," the man shrugged as if to cast me off. "But everyone says the same. I'm only saying what everyone says."

I looked back at my Auntie's face at the window. I looked back at the idiot man, with his round, turnip head and his blank-faced wife. I looked at his horrendous children and his ugly baby. Thank God I'm not related to these morons, I thought.

"It's what everyone says," his nothing wife mumbled. "It really is."

I turned the full force of my stare onto her. "You should know that I cannot accept anything that you say for one reason and one reason only," I said.

Throwing Stones

NOBODY LIKED BERNARD BOYLE. He kept himself to himself, except for occasionally shouting at children who got noisy as they scooted up and down the street.

"Watch it!" He'd point his meaty fingers at them to make it clear exactly at whom his threat was directed. "I know where you live," he'd say.

Three generations of children in Tanner Street had known the terrifying regularity of nightmares starring Bernard Boyle and his jabby fingers and spittle-flecked lips.

"You there! Yes, you! I'm talking to *you*! Keep it *down!*" He'd slam his window shut and the children in the street would exchange a look of fear or loathing, depending on their age. When they got home, they'd complain about him to their mothers, who would bat it away with a wave of their hand. "Just ignore him. He's a lonely, sad old man whose wife left him," the more charitable mothers would say.

Bernard lived his days between the World War II channel and his online chess career. He had been exceptional at chess since learning to play in his teens. Those he played didn't know him from Adam. His opponents were Dutch, Korean, Russian, Canadian... the international language of chess knew no boundaries, and people all over the world had lost money to Bernard Boyle.

The good thing about the Corona virus, Bernard kept thinking to himself latterly, was that it had brought a whole new crowd of fools into the online chess arena. Fresh meat, keen to have a go, happy to risk £50 against – they assumed – a fellow player of average intelligence and ability. In the last three days, Bernard had made almost £2,000, thanks to the virus. By the end of this, when it was all over, he expected to be in the tens of thousands. This whole solitary confinement thing could go on forever, so far as Bernard was concerned.

When he first heard the commotion outside, he ignored it. Probably just a fight kicking off, he thought, pouring himself a second glass of whisky.

But the shouting continued. Perhaps it was someone being attacked, he thought: in which case, better to ignore it. He turned back to his computer screen, where he was mid-game with some complete amateur. He wondered whether to put them into check, or string them along for a few more moves.

The shouting grew louder. Bernard Boyle decided to cash in on the game and look out of his window. He tapped his queen six spaces along the diagonal to complete a checkmate, clicked his mouse, and, as if by magic, the money was in his account. He didn't bother exchanging congratulations or commiserations with his opponent, but instead went and opened his front door to discover the source of the commotion.

A group of people were gathered around the front of a house four doors down from Bernard Boyle. They were shouting and screaming and banging on the doors and windows. Bernard strained his ears to distinguish their words, but he couldn't make them out.

He grabbed a door key, turned off his lounge light and stepped out of his house, into the darkness of the street. As he walked towards the crowd, several of them turned to look at him, their faces still shouting angry accusations at the 1930s semi before them.

"What's going on?" Bernard asked a woman with greying brown hair and a thick cardigan on.

"They're hoarders," she replied. "Bloody hoarders."

"What?"

"I saw him myself," she said. "He'd been to Asda, Sainsbury's, Morrison's and Tesco's, and he's bought masses of toilet roll at every single one of them. I saw him myself, heaving it all back in here. Enough to wipe his arse for five years."

Bernard stared at the house in disbelief.

"I'm down to my last four rolls," he said.

"I've only got six rolls in, and I've got kids," the woman replied.

"Bastard!" Bernard said, spittle hitting the coat sleeve of the woman, who winced and stepped back a little. "The dirty, selfish bastard."

"Exactly," she said, raising her voice to cover the distance between them. "It's disgraceful. People like this need to be called out."

"They do indeed. And they will." Bernard Boyle stepped forward, and peered over the low front fence into the gravelled front garden. Reaching down between two clumps of daffodils, he picked up a stone, and threw it at the front windows.

"Yeah!" the woman shouted, pushing forward to join him. "Selfish bastard! Take that!"

Bernard had never felt so much solidarity with another human. He had never felt such acceptance in a group. Nobody here cared about social distancing: they were united in a cause.

The curtains parted slightly in the bay window, and a sheet of A4 paper was held up.

"What does it say?" someone asked. The group screwed their eyes up and tried to read.

"It says he's buying them for other people," someone said. The group fell quiet for a moment.

"Bollocks," Bernard said.

"Yeah, that's gotta be. Who does that?"

"Yeah, liar!" came a stronger voice.

"Liar!" began the chant, gathering volume. "Liar! Liar! Liar!"

Bernard picked up another stone and threw it.

A LEARNING OPPORTUNITY

"I CAN'T TALK NOW, MUM, I'm supposed to be doing the creative writing tutorial," Martha said.

Her mother sighed. "Well you couldn't talk earlier because you were doing the fitness session."

"I'll call you later," Martha said. "Love you."

But she didn't call her later. She'd forgotten that she'd signed up for the online Italian course, which began that evening.

It had only been two weeks since the lockdown, and already Martha Lacey had signed up for twelve online learning and activity groups.

At 9am, she began the day with a fitness session. 9.30 was a local choir which involved standing in the bath, singing into a shower head on a Zoom meeting, so that you could see lots of other people singing into their own shower heads. It had been fun for a few days, but now it was starting to feel like a bit of an effort to climb into the bath, fully dressed.

Anyway, at 10.30 every day she'd begun to do the creative writing course she'd signed up for, which was being run by a publishing company. Each day they set a task that should mean that, by the end of the self-isolation period, she should have the first draft of a novel completed. She'd started well, but had been falling behind every day since day two. She'd got the beginning roughed out, the ending loosely jotted in a list form, but still no idea about the big, soupy mass in the middle. Her characters were not as fully fleshed as she'd been promised they would be by now, and she was losing heart, a little. But this was her chance. She would never have an opportunity like this again!

She'd ordered three novels this morning before breakfast, via Amazon. She'd always meant to try Russian writers, and here was her chance, at last. She gave a sideways glance at the pile of books that had been slowly rising by the side of her bed over the last year. The new novels she'd ordered today were the ones she was really keen to read. When she'd finished them, she'd finally crack onto that old pile.

At 10:05, singing over with, she checked her mobile. In the half hour she'd been standing in the bath, 59 WhatsApp messages had come in, and her Facebook notification showed 72 messages for her to catch up with.

The street WhatsApp group she'd joined to keep up with her immediate neighbours showed that she'd missed social distance circuit training about twenty minutes ago. She'd been in the shower, self-consciously attempting Tina Turner at the time.

She put the kettle on to boil, and worried all the time that she made and drank her tea that the whole street must think her antisocial. Also, she hadn't added to the word count of the novel she'd never finish.

There wasn't much time to worry about it, though, because she'd signed up to a Japanese cookery session via YouTube and was making lunch live, alongside a top chef. She'd got some of the ingredients, and was fairly confident she could improvise where necessary.

As it turned out, you couldn't replace bread for tofu to great effect. Still, it was a terrific learning opportunity.

Cooking an inedible lunch had made her hungry, but upon opening her cupboard doors she discovered that she didn't really have anything in that grabbed her. She had better go out and top up on supplies. She took an envelope from the recycling bin and made a list:

Eggs
Flour
Loo roll
Bread
Cadbury's FnN or Caramel
Apples
Choc digestives
Butter
Cheese
Wool
Art materials
Yoga mat
Lycra running bottoms
Crochet hook
Knitting needles
Paintbrushes
Set of drawing pencils
Clay
Chicken wire
Drawing paper
Watercolour pad
Notebooks
Bedding plants
Compost bag
Gro-bag

Tomato seeds
Lettuce seeds

That should see her through the next week. By summer, thanks to the gro-bag, she should be virtually self-sufficient and less dependent on the supermarkets. At least, that's what the blog she'd just subscribed to had said.

It took seven supermarkets before she managed to find most of the things on her list, and upon unpacking it in her kitchen, Martha was depressed to see that the only edible she'd managed to get hold of was a squashed little loaf of tiger bread. Looking at its rippled, crusty pattern reminded her that she'd missed the first session of the online traditional fair-isle knitting course she'd signed up for. She'd never catch up, now!

She sat down on her kitchen floor and stared at the washing-machine door for a few minutes, feeling completely stamped out by all that she should be doing and wasn't.

Perhaps she ought to go for a walk around the block. She hadn't done that yet today. It might clear her head.

She got her coat and scarf out, and dug her gloves out. Wrapping the scarf around the lower half of her face, she set out down her street.

Normally a thoroughfare to town, her street would have been busy. But today, all was still. It felt like Christmas day, or an apocalypse. As she turned onto the main road, she looked around: no cars. The silence was eerie. She felt her phone buzz in her pocket and saw a message from a friend requesting a WhatsApp video call to share coffee and a catch up: just when was she supposed to fit that in?

She looked up. A man was walking towards her. He was about a hundred metres from her at the moment, walking and reading his phone screen. He glanced up and saw her, froze for the slightest moment, then turned and crossed the road so that he was well away from her when they passed one another. She knew it was sensible, yet somehow still felt offended by it, as if she had been rejected. She wanted to scream, "I don't have it!" But then the thought occurred that perhaps he *did* have it, and so perhaps she should call out a thank you.

The street was so quiet that she could hear his right shoe, which squeaked every time he put that foot down. That must drive him crazy, she thought.

The newsagents was open. Perhaps they would have a pint of milk. Using her elbow and shoulder, she pushed the door open.

"Hello," the man behind the counter smiled from behind his face mask, and raised a blue-latex-gloved hand in greeting.

"Hello," Martha said, feeling the jolt of unexpected pleasure at human interaction.

"Alright?"

"I'm fine, thanks. All healthy," said Martha. "You?"

"Yeah, I'm fine."

It felt as if they had both passed a little test.

"I don't suppose you've got any milk in?" Martha said.

"Sure do," the man replied. "I've got loads of everything."

She turned sharply, her mouth open. "No way!"

"Yep. Bread. Eggs. You name it."

"Free range?"

"Yep. I get them from Grange Farm. They're bringing me a daily delivery at the moment."

"Wow! You don't have flour though, do you?"

"Plain or self-raising?"

"You have a choice?"

"Yep. I've got both."

"How come you're so well stocked?"

"Coz everyone thinks food only comes from Tesco's these days," the man said, smiling. "They think we only sell sweets and fags and Special Brew. Luckily for you, right?"

"Too right." Martha filled a bag with eggs, milk, flour, cheese, butter, tins of beans and soup, porridge oats, fresh orange juice and loo roll. "That's amazing," she said, as the shopkeeper opened the door with his gloved hand to let her out. She really felt as if she'd got a bag of treasure, and couldn't stop smiling all the way home.

But when she opened the front door, all the to-do's lurched back at her. The phone began to ring and Martha found herself feeling tearful.

"I'm going to have a bath," she said out loud. "No one can get you in the bath."

As the water ran, Martha cast her eye down the list of things she was missing: a lecture on some underground tunnels in the Midlands; a free viewing of Cats the musical; she saw that Gordon Ramsey had launched an app where you could live stream him into your kitchen and cook while he shouted insults at you.

"Not on your Nelly," Martha said.

The bath was full, with a foamy cloud of bubbles on it, like a beer with a perfect head. If only she already had the novels she'd ordered this morning! But who knew when they might arrive?

The first book on the pile by her bed was *A Tale Of Two Cities*, by Charles Dickens. She had always meant to read

Dickens. And yet, somehow this novel that she once claimed to yearn to read had been sitting by the bed for almost a year, untouched. She ran her hand over its cover, turning the book in her hands to look at the spine. She flipped through the pages with her thumb, then took it from the bedroom to the bathroom and placed it on the window ledge above the bath. Surveying the scene, she realised what was missing: a cup of tea.

She made one in her biggest mug, and, as she lay in the bath, she reached for the Dickens and read the opening lines. She held the mug on her chest, feeling the heat of her tea through the bubble bath foam. She closed her eyes and, at last, exhaled.

PETER AND PAUL

FROM BEHIND THE GREYING LACE CURTAINS of number fifteen, Peter could observe the whole of Lyle Street, from the first, pristine Victorian semi with its grey paintwork and potted bay trees, all the way along to the brown bungalow built after the war on a bombsite, with its garish garden gnomes armed with fishing rods and rakes.

As he peered through the weary veil, the front door of the house opposite Peter's opened, and the front legs of a walking frame emerged from the dark unknown into the glaring sunlight. Edna, with her short, spiky hair stepped out, dragging her short, spiky dog – yapping in complaint, as ever – behind her.

"Out for a poo," Peter said, to no one.

It had been two weeks, apparently, since the social isolation had been enforced. The numbers were mesmerising; Peter sat in front of the telly, reading the strip that ran continuously across the bottom of the screen. The statistics told the stories of thousands being tested, while just hundreds had been found to have the disease. According to the news, these numbers had brought the NHS to its knees already, and there was talk of ice rinks being used as morgues and new hospitals being built at top speed to cope. Peter stared at the text running across his screen in terrified, frozen fascination. Each day he stared, reading them backwards and forwards as if it were some sort of awful lottery that he wasn't sure if he had bought a ticket for, but watched just in case his number got called out.

"It can't be me," Peter said, to no one, as he ran an antibacterial wipe over the shopping that Ocado had just delivered. Peter hadn't left the house in almost two years. Once a week, he had two loaves of bread, twenty four eggs, a block of butter, eight pints of milk, a jar of coffee and eight ready meals and a bunch of bananas delivered to his door. He cut his own hair and took great care of his teeth. He hadn't been to the doctor's or a dentist in half a decade.

About a year ago, Julia, the woman from next door, had knocked and called through the letterbox.

"Are you alright in there, Peter?"

She'd been in the street as long as anyone, and had been friends with Peter's mother. He remembered them talking over the fence. She'd known his brother, Paul, too.

She'd kept banging the knocker and worrying at the letterbox, calling, "Peter? Peter? Peter?"

Eventually he'd had to call back.

"I'm fine," was all he'd said.

But it hadn't got rid of her as he'd hoped. "If you need anything, you know where I am," she called in her high voice. "Is your brother alright? Have you heard from him?" Of course, she must have heard the way Paul left the house eighteen months ago, shouting and slamming doors.

"I'm fine," Peter replied. Moments later, from where he sat on the floor by the front door, so close that he could feel a draft through the keyhole, he heard her sigh as she retreated, back to her own house. He heard her front door closing, a faint thud through the wall of his lounge.

He'd written to Paul a year and two months ago, but the silence returned daily. Sometimes it was unbearable, the silence from Paul. It screamed accusations that Peter found himself denying to an empty house.

It was eleven o'clock. Peter went to get a banana from the packet on the kitchen table. He sat and ate it, breaking the soft flesh by pushing it up against the roof of his mouth. "Don't play with your food, Peter," he imagined his mother saying.

The faintest tap at the back door announced the arrival of the ginger cat, as her tail hit the glass. Peter, glad to be pulled from the memory, stuffed the last of the banana into his cheek like a hamster and opened the door.

"Hello, Mrs. Cat," he said, as the well-fed creature wrapped itself around his legs, circling his shins in an affectionate dance, its thin tail rising towards Peter's knee. "Hello," he reached down and pushed his fingers into the thick, soft fur. "Love you, Mrs. Cat," he tickled behind her ears and under her chin, and she purred brightly.

This had been going on for some months now. Peter had no idea which house Mrs. Cat belonged to. He went to the cupboard, almost tripping as Mrs. Cat wound herself faster and faster around his legs. "It's coming, don't fret," he soothed, reaching for a packet of *Dreamies*. He got a bowl and tipped the food in. Mrs. Cat yowled as she always did, before digging in. "You're welcome," Peter said. He stood and listened to the sounds of Mrs. Cat's tongue and teeth at work, clicking and smacking until the job was done, then licking the bowl dry.

She looked up at him. "You're very welcome," he said again. He reached for her, and cupped her head in his hand, running his thumb back and forth over her soft cheek. "I love you," he said. She purred.

She followed him down the hall, back to the lounge, where he sat on the armchair in the bay, and she settled onto his lap, pushing and kneading his legs with her fat paws for a moment before settling.

Peter was stroking Mrs. Cat, admiring the tigery ripples of dark and pale ginger on her back, when the postman walked up the front path. From his secret space behind the net curtain, he watched as the postman sorted through a small pile and pushed it through Peter's letterbox.

As the postman walked away, Peter saw Edna returning from her walk, small black poo-bag dangling from her hand. He watched the bag swinging heavily, banging against the steel of her walking frame. It looked full. Hard to believe sometime so large and rounded could have come from such a tiny, spiky creature. Peter imagined Edna picking up the wrong poo – something from a Saint Bernard – leaving her own dog's pin-sized pellets behind for a confused Saint Bernard owner to collect.

There were people in the street again. This was what he'd been waiting to watch. Each day of the confinement so far, people from Lyle Street had taken their mugs outside and stood around, sipping, keeping their distance, chatting to one another across the road. It had been interesting to see people – people he used to say good morning to, back when he'd gone to work and Mother had been well and Paul had been talking to him.

"Do you belong to one of them?" Peter asked Mrs. Cat, who blinked and kept her eyes tight shut and refused to answer. "I reckon that means yes," Peter said.

Edna was standing at the end of her path, her trembling dog yapping at her ankles, straining at the leash to get back indoors. But Edna was chatting, and laughing, even, with Mrs. Campervan and Mr. Hanging Baskets.

Peter had read the note they'd pushed through his door: mid-morning coffee in the street. Keep your social distance while having a chat. He'd watched them every morning, all those people his mother had been on such friendly terms with, and some who'd moved in since she'd gone. He wondered if she'd have made friends with Mrs. Campervan: of course she would. She was friends with the whole world. Quite the opposite of father.

"Sometimes, I wish," Peter said to Mrs. Cat, but she just purred and pushed into his lap. "Come on," he began to move. "Let's see what bills I've got today." Carefully, Peter moved ever so slightly. Mrs. Cat understood, rose and hopped lightly to the floor, landing with dignified solidity and heading for the hallway.

There was something from Specsavers, something from the council, a flyer from Ocado offering money off to new customers (which Peter angrily screwed into a ball) and then, a postcard from London. Peter held his breath as he turned it over. There was his brother's scrawl; there was his brother's name. Mrs. Cat watched Peter as a tear ran from his face and sploshed on the floor by her paw.

"It wasn't your fault," the postcard said. "No one saw the signs. I don't blame you anymore. Call me, if you still want to."

Peter stood very still. Mrs. Cat mewed. He looked at her. He read the card again. She mewed and pushed her cheek against his shin. He smiled a little. She pushed again. He reached down and gave her the comfort she was asking for. She mewed in pleasure and seemed to lift her face towards the front door.

Peter stood and slipped the postcard into his back pocket. He took a deep breath, lifted his mug for a bolstering sip and then opened the door.

KING OF THE ROAD

FOR THE FIRST TIME IN MY LIFE, mine is the only car on the ring-road, and it feels tremendous. I put my foot down, harder still, and thrill to the force of speed that I feel first as a faint tingle in my groin. I'm like the star in a car advert. I really do *own* the road right now.

The steering wheel beneath my fingers responds beautifully to the lightest touch. I zigzag the empty lanes for fun, criss-crossing the lines that normally force me to submit.

"I run this town!" I shout, laughing – but it really does seem like I do, truth be told. I jack my stereo up and soak up the fantastic sounds of the James Bond theme tune. The bass timbre sweeps and blasts into every luxurious corner of the car's interior, bouncing off the walnut dash and caressing the leather seats like a silk glove.

"I'm the king of the world!" I shout at a blackbird that must have been dared by another blackbird to fly right across my path, dangerously close to my vast windscreen.

If there's an upside to this Corona thing, then surely this is it. No more idiots on the road, I can cruise and text knowing that I won't get done. It's all mine for the taking. Only the brave venture out anywhere further than Tesco's, now. It's almost as if I've been waiting for this moment to begin to truly live as I choose.

I swing the car around a bend and feel the lurch in my gut as gravity pulls me one way and the machine fights back. I'm doing a lap of the ring road. I would normally turn off here, but my mind is made up. And, let's face it, there's no rules anymore. I might do laps all day, so long as no one else is bothering the tarmac.

I sweep majestically into a short strait, and follow the curve of a roundabout without pausing. There's no need. The road is mine. I think to myself, I'm going to do a circuit around this roundabout. I'm going to put a ring around it and claim it as my own. "Yes!" I shout, and again, "Yes!" I'm in full flow and no one is having better ideas than me.

I lean in and pull tightly down on the wheel. The car does my bidding, machine and man in perfect harmony. And round we go, like a fairground pleasure ride.

There are blossomy trees on the roundabout, and petals scatter across my windscreen like confetti, and I think, I'm happier right now than I was on my first wedding day. This is the moment of my life. This is me at the wheel and I am unstoppable!

A flash of blue and red catches my eye. As I go round I see it again. There in the middle of the roundabout. What is it? I'm going too fast to be able to focus. A bag? Is it a bag caught in the scrubby bushes on the middle of the roundabout? I circle again, slowing a little. I'm like a great, powerful shark circling some dumb little fish, closing in.

It's a woman!

There is a woman, standing on the roundabout in a red jumper and blue jeans. She's looking at the trees, but she sees me also. She feels my power against her fragile frame.

She's quite attractive.

I honk my horn.

She waves and smiles.

"What are you doing?" I shout, pleased with how good my teeth are.

She says something, but I can't catch it. Eventually I have to stop. There's no one around, so I park up against the roundabout.

She doesn't look so happy now. Her smile is gone. She backs away from the centre, away from the side I have parked on.

"What are you doing?" I call.

"Sorry," she replies. "I guess I'm not supposed to be here."

"Why not?" I say.

She smiles just a little, but she's nervous. I can see it. "I thought I'd come here while I could. I mean, when else can one get to a roundabout on foot in the middle of the morning?"

"Yes," I say, an idea forming in my mind. "You're right."

I get back in my car and drive away. I sweep one more glorious lap of honour around the ring road, and when I pass the roundabout again, she's gone.

Back home, I head for the garage. I take thick garden canes and old tent fabric. I find gloss paint. I daub my initials upon the fabric. I find my mallet. I find duck-tape and secure the fabric to the canes. I load it all into my deceptively spacious boot and off I go.

I stop at the first roundabout and, rather than drive around it, I mount the car straight up onto it. With my mallet I hammer my flag into the earthy centre of the roundabout. I raise my hands, fists clenched. I shout, "Mine!"

I get back into the car and cruise to the next roundabout, and round the ring road to the next, and the next, until all eight roundabouts bear my mark, like a royal standard.

Next time she thinks about mucking about on roundabouts, she'll know whose permission she needs to ask: Mine. The King of the Road.

THE FLOW

FOR THE FIRST WEEK OR SO it had been all soups and stews. Eva had peeled and diced, checked and stirred, added a dash of wine or a splash of cream. She'd picked fresh herbs from the garden, or dried herbs from the cupboard. Everything seemed to begin with onions, carrots and celery. She'd toasted croutons, made by chopping the crusts of bread and tossing them in olive oil, sweet smoked paprika and garlic granules, spreading them out on a baking sheet and shutting them into a hot oven for ten minutes. The smells that filled the house were heavenly, but when it came to the eating, she barely tasted the food.

Her husband and children were always slow in coming to the table. She'd call out that dinner was nearly ready about thirty seconds after she began chopping the onions. She'd give them two more warnings, five minutes and then two minutes before the food was ready, like an invigilator in the last moments of an exam.

Still, no one came, and so, while the food congealed, dried out, burned or grew cold, she would head off around the house to hunt them out. Actually, it wasn't much of a game of hide and seek: she knew exactly where each of them would be. Summer would be in her room, watching Netflix on her laptop; Sadie would be in her corner of the same room, phone in hand, earphones in, listening to music or watching YouTube videos; Oscar would be on his beanbag, in front of the PS4, headphones on and mouthpiece wrapped around his cheek, chatting to friends whilst running around shooting things, and Gavin... well, Gavin would most likely be upstairs, sitting on their bed (banished from the lounge by his teenage son), reading the news on the iPad. She had, twice, walked in on him sitting on the toilet, reading the news on the iPad.

Gavin had become obsessed by the news. Each evening, he recited all the gloom that he had absorbed and dragged her down into the awful pit where one view of reality trumped all others.

"There must be other things going on in the world," Eva said, knowing already what his answer would be.

"Nope. Nothing worth reporting on, anyway, otherwise they'd report on it, wouldn't they? There's really only one story in the world right now, Eva, and that's Corona."

"Surely some old lady somewhere lost a cat twelve years ago, only to have it mysteriously saunter through her back door as if nothing had happened. Surely that's happened *somewhere* in the world?"

"No, because all the old ladies in the world have their back and front doors firmly shut because they are self-isolating."

"But there must be a natural phenomenon carrying on somewhere. An earthquake or a volcano or something. Not that I would wish that on anybody."

"It seems as if all seismic activity must be on hold until the current crisis passes. And nobody knows when that will be. Especially now that Boris is unwell. I reckon he's got it."

"He might just be exhausted, and run down. He might just have a tired throat."

"There's no such thing as a tired throat anymore, Eva," he said all this while swiping his finger across the iPad screen, "There is only Corona. The common cold is dead."

"Well, anyway, tea's on the table," Eva would say, rolling her eyes as she headed back downstairs, calling loudly that tea was ready to anyone who might hear her on her way.

Each evening she sat by her plate and waited for them all. She didn't dish up until they arrived. She watched the steam from the food dwindling. Eventually, reluctantly, they emerged from their caves, each blinking bloodshot eyes.

"You'll all need glasses when this is over," Eva said, regularly enough to make them each tut and roll their eyes by now. "The opticians are going to make a killing, when we finally get back to normal."

"Well, I don't know when that will be," Gavin said. "They should probably start devising ways to test eyes online because we're a very long way off normal, from what I'm reading. Especially now that Boris has got it."

"You don't know for sure that he's got it," Eva shot Gavin a look. She was increasingly worried about making the children anxious. To hear that the person in charge of everything wasn't safe might alarm them unnecessarily.

"Nah, he's got it," Oscar said, casually reaching for the mashed potato and letting a weighty spoonful of it land with a satisfying whump on his plate.

"Definitely? How do you know?" Gavin straightened in his dining chair, pulled closer into the table, "If he had, I should know. I've been on the BBC all afternoon."

"Hmmm," Eva said, quietly, lips pursed as she reached for the broccoli.

"I heard it from Tyler. We were playing Fortnite."

"Oh, well, it's just his word, then."

"No, it's confirmed."

Gavin took his phone from his pocket and began to scroll.

"No phones at the table, *Dad*!" Sadie said, her eyes on Mum, the regular enforcer of that rule.

Eva sighed and helped herself to a spoonful of carrots, laying them on her plate alongside the coq au vin that she'd spent the last ninety minutes creating. She looked at the way Summer was picking at her food and pushing it around her plate in the hopes of making it somehow go away without her having to put any of it in her actual mouth. Sadie wrinkled her nose in disgust and simply said, "Carrots. Ew." Gavin ate as if he were being paid to do it on a piecemeal basis, and she knew his focus was on getting the plate finished so that he might get back to the BBC and find out every scrap of information available about Boris's latest health status update. Oscar tucked in fast, barely chewing, filling his mouth as if it were a race.

"I need to get back to the game," he said, already half out of his seat.

"What do you say to Mum?" Gavin said, eyes fixed on the carrot stick he was chasing around his plate.

"Thanks," Oscar replied, already at the door and on his way back to the lounge. For a fraction of a second he caught Eva's eye, and then he was gone.

"I really do want to be a vegetarian, you know," Summer used her brother's exit to get up, taking her plate, assuming her Mother hadn't noticed all the coq au vin that remained uneaten. She hummed a pop song loudly to cover the sounds made by scraping her food into the bin.

"Yeah, I'm done," Sadie got up, too. "Thanks and all that." She pushed behind Summer, keen to dispose of her own leftovers.

"I can see both of you perfectly well," Eva said, her mouth full of the congealed, cold chicken stew that had been so fiddly to make.

"Thanks, Mum," the girls chorused, smiling as if one thank you from them could make everything alright. Eva gave a half-smile: it worked a bit, but only a bit.

Gavin swallowed his last mouthful. "That was great, love," he said, taking his empty plate to the dishwasher. "Thanks." He squeezed her shoulder as he passed by on his way back to the bedroom.

Eva sat, alone, with the dirty serving bowls, trying to work out how this pattern had established itself so quickly and so firmly. According to Facebook, her friends' families were baking, crafting, gardening and letter-writing together. The only ones in their homes who seemed to be on any sort of technology were the mothers who posted the awesome photos of sibling harmony and wholesome activity onto Facebook. She'd reached the stage already where she could hardly bare to look anymore. It was just too painful a mirror to hold up, and she couldn't stand the reflection it presented her with.

She reached for the vegetable dish and placed it inside the larger stew pot. Turning to the kitchen behind her, she was shocked to see Oscar had returned, unheard. He was in the stealthy process of stealing a Snickers bar from the cupboard. His hand moved slowly so as not to disturb any of the other biscuits in that cupboard.

"I'm right behind you," Eva said, which produced a very satisfying little jump on Oscar's part. "If you were still hungry, you should have taken more mash. There's still some left over. Do you want some?"

Oscar looked towards his escape route. "That's ok, thanks Mum," he said, putting on that sweet baby smile of his which so often succeeded in getting him his own way. "Bye, love you." He slipped out of the room and returned to the lounge and his game.

Eva stood there, in the middle of the kitchen, staring at the pile of dishes and the grubby, finger-marked units, and the open bin lid, and she began to cry. Not with loud sobs, but in silence, her mouth open and no sound coming out. At first, the tears rolled freely down her face and fell onto the lino with tiny mouse-splashes.

"How did this happen?" she whisper-wheezed the words to the empty room, and then, "How much longer?"

No one seemed to know the answer to this, no matter how much news they read or how many online chats they took part in.

But the weather changed from soups and stews to salads and sandwiches. Eva waited in supermarket queues, worrying about whether the people either side of her were closer than two metres. She made her way around the shops in as little time as possible, her scarf around her face and her alcohol gel in her pocket. When she got home, she wiped down each and every item with antibacterial wipes, never quite putting her mind at rest before she stowed things away in the cupboards.

She bought Quorn fillets in an effort to please Summer's vegetarian aspirations. She bought steak because a slab of steak always cheered Gavin up. She topped up on Snickers bars for Oscar and didn't buy any more carrots for Sadie's sake. She thought that if she lived alone, she would just buy bread and butter and apples, and to hell with all the rest of it.

By now, Boris was really ill. Each day, Gavin kept her updated on his condition, as if the Prime Minister were a member of their own family. She found herself one time on her knees, scrubbing down the side of the toilet base, praying for Boris's swift recovery.

Mother's day had been and gone, back at the beginning of all this. At that point, Gavin had announced that the lockdown measures imposed would be lifted in a few days, and they could easily delay their celebration and take Eva out for afternoon tea somewhere, probably killing two birds with one stone and combining it with a visit to his mother's. Eva, thinking that was an unlikely scenario in the next few days, didn't bother to give an opinion which would only offend.

As the weeks went on and the weather changed, Eva began to create pictures in her mind of what she would like to do, given the choice. Gone were the foolish notions of family harmony. They'd vanished the afternoon she'd turned the broadband off.

She'd had this notion that without Wifi, the family might be forced to come together. She had pictured jigsawing, and board games, digging a vegetable patch or learning to identify birdsong together. Instead she had witnessed scenes of breakdown, rioting and looting of the kitchen cupboards. Her family had spent twenty minutes tearing through the house, hands to their cheeks, faces resembling Eduard Munch's traumatised screamer, before Oscar had noticed that the switch on the box was off. Peace returned instantly, the way it does when a dummy is plugged into the mouth of a screaming baby.

Eva slowly progressed through the house, emptying cupboards and filling boxes for – eventual – charity donations. She filled the recycling bin with old, forgotten piles of birthday cards and pizza menus. She swung the vacuum hose in the air and followed hitherto unnoticed trails of cobwebs across ceilings, wondering where all these spiders that had clearly been so busy, could be now. She descaled the kettle, defrosted the freezer and cleaned out the fridge. She worked her way down a list of things that had been bothering her for years. She marvelled at how satisfying it was to see clearly the contents of a cupboard or drawer upon opening it, and to be able to find things so quickly.

Slowly, steadily, an order returned to the house that she hadn't known since before Summer was born. And all the time, she queued, she shopped, she cooked, she fed, she cleared up. But something was growing within her. The house was finally looking the way she liked it. The boot of the car was loaded with bags and boxes for charity. The front garden was tidy, with all the weeds gone and a lavender bush donated by a neighbour, settling happily into the blank space by the front gate that she'd meant to fill for years.

There was always cleaning to do. Always laundry to wash, dry, iron and put away. Always meals to make and treats to bake. Always someone needing an audience to moan to about their news, their irritating friends, the pathetic data allowance on their phone or the useless broadband speed in this house.

Once or twice, Eva spent an afternoon on Facebook on her own phone. It left her feeling overwhelmed by the constant lists of suggested activities and groups to join, and depressed by the postings of people she half knew whose children were doing sociable and impressive things. She soon stopped looking.

Then, one morning, a solution struck her. She was reaching for the biscuit cupboard, wishing that she had the strength to resist a custard cream, when her husband appeared in the kitchen.

"Caught red-handed," he said, feeling that he'd made a mutually pleasing joke.

"I know," Eva set her mouth firmly and folded her arms. "I do realise I'm gaining a bit of weight. I can feel it in my jeans. All my clothes, actually. They're all feeling a bit tighter."

"Well you *are* spending an awful lot of time in the kitchen," Gavin said. "You're like a kid in a sweetshop in here." He grabbed the last Snickers and headed upstairs, calling over his shoulder as he went, "What you need is to do your daily exercise while you still can. They're talking about banning that, now. We won't even be allowed out for a walk."

"We haven't been going out for walks!" Eva called up, but Gavin was in the bedroom now, settling back onto the bed with the iPad.

Eva was hurt. She'd said she was fat and he hadn't contradicted her. He hadn't told her she was beautiful and desirable. He hadn't touched her. He hadn't said he loved her. She tried to remember the last time they'd been intimate, and found herself unable to pinpoint whether it had been before or after Christmas.

She headed to the freshly cleared-through and organised coat cupboard, and took some small pleasure in how easily she found her light summer jacket.

"I'm going for a walk," she called. No one answered, so she shouted it this time. "I'M GOING FOR A WALK!" A couple of vague Ok sounds acknowledged her just enough to set her conscience straight that she *had* told them, so she took the door keys and stepped out into the big bad world.

The sky was a bright, pale blue, unsullied by clouds. Birds sang, lawnmowers purred, and in a garden somewhere, strange music twanged discordantly into the air. She breathed in deeply, then, worried by the thought that the virus might be floating around her, she began to walk.

In five minutes, she was on the main road. She could go right, into town, or left, towards the river. She went left. Along the main road, with its chip shop, Chinese takeaway, newsagents and pet shop; past the red brick old people's home where carers came and went and it appeared from the outside to be business as usual; past the dog groomers and the nail salon, both looking emptier somehow than if they were merely closed for lunch.

Lunch!

She headed back to the newsagents – the only shop open between here and the river – and bought a bag of pickled onion Monster Munch and a can of Diet Coke. The shopkeeper was friendly, and displayed no outward signs of ill-health.

Back on the road, she took the small bottle of alcohol gel from her pocket and rubbed it all over her hands and rubbed her hands over the crisp packet and Coke can. Then, she headed for the river, excited at the thought of the picnic in the brown paper bag that she now carried. A woman walked ahead of her, and she made sure she held her speed and distance steady.

There was another woman walking on the other side of the street, headed in the same direction. Eva glanced across: they were keeping exactly the same pace. The woman noticed it, too, and turned and smiled at Eva in acknowledgement. Eva felt an instant connection and was sad that they couldn't be side by side.

She walked on. Each step took her farther from home. One walk could last many hours, she thought. They'd limited the number of walks you took, but not the length of time for each walk. She found she was gaining on the woman in front, and she had no wish to slow down. The speed was good. She checked over her shoulder: the road was empty. She crossed into the middle of the road, placing herself between the women either side of her, and marched on. She was walking to the river. She would find a good space on the river bank and she would drink her Coke and eat her Monster Munch and the water would run freely and lightly past and all would be well, and all would be well, and all manner of thing would be well.

She was picking up pace with each stride, her heart pumping quicker, her pulse tripping brightly, her mind fresh as if new air had pushed out all the old. Her thoughts seemed clearer, out here, away from all the invisible electronic signals that bounced off every surface in her home. She overtook the woman to her right, and she passed five more women and one man before she made the final turn, down the side of the park and ride carpark, into the river and its marshes. As she crossed the broad bridge over to the other side of the river, where a path led all the way to town in one direction and all the way to open country and pretty villages in the other, she stopped, blinking rapidly, in an effort to take in the scene before her.

The river path was full of women, walking. Each one of them bore the smile of a child on its first day of the summer holidays. As she watched, she began to pick out a few men in the crowd, dotted here and there, but overwhelmingly it was women, as far as the eye could see. Perhaps two or three hundred women, all walking and smiling. Greetings were exchanged across the gaps between them. Some were doing yoga on the marshes. Some sat on the river bank, with books and magazines. Some dipped fingers into the water, enjoying its coolness on their skin. Some walked dogs. Some wore full on fitness gear, while one or two looked as if they might be in pyjamas. Many carried sandals and walked barefoot on the grass. There were sunhats and a few parasols. It looked like a parade, a pageant, a festival…

"Excuse me?" A voice behind Eva made her turn around. The first woman she'd smiled at was waiting about two metres behind her, and she saw now that, behind that woman, was another, and another – all waiting for her to move forward. "Are you going in?" The woman asked, still smiling.

"I'm so sorry," Eva said. "I am. It's my first time here. So many women!"

"Yeah, and we all know why *that* is," an older woman further back in the queue said, laughing. Others laughed, too.

"We're stepping into the flow!" came a shout from down the line.

"Recharging," said another.

The woman behind her nodded. "If you walk long enough, you'll find yourself travelling within a flow of power," she said. "It's invisible, but it's definitely real, and it runs all the way along the river, through the crowd. You'll sense it, I promise."

Eva began to walk. She took the path to the left, and walked amongst the women, all the way to the second village.

All the way, a sense of lightness coursed through her body and mind. There was an energy in her limbs and a joyful beat in her spirit that made her want to sing – so she did. She walked and sang: pop songs, Christmas carols and nursery rhymes. She sang out of tune and she didn't care.

"I should bring my family here," she thought, her mind immediately hearing all the protestations such a suggestion would certainly rouse. The sounds in her head immediately exhausted her. Her legs ached, and she felt dusty. She suddenly felt that it was wrong of her, selfish to be out here enjoying this alone. She decided to turn back and head for home, and a shower.

The moment she inserted her key into the front door, it was pulled open from the inside by a very harassed looking Gavin.

"Where have you been?"

"I told you, I went for a walk."

"That was five hours ago!" he said, hands held out in exasperation. "You missed lunch and none of us knew where anything was."

"You say that like it's my fault," she replied. "Did you manage to work out that the bread is in the metal box marked 'bread', and the cheese is in the fridge?"

"Eventually," Gavin said, having the decency to blush a little, "But we couldn't find the crisps."

"They're in the same cupboard as the Snickers. I'd've thought you'd have noticed them." Eva sighed.

"Well, anyway," Gavin blustered, "We've made tea. We're all in the dining room, waiting for you right now."

Eva stopped where she was in the hallway, halfway through hanging up her jacket. "Really? You made tea?" She sniffed the air, but detected no cooking smells.

"Yes. We've been waiting for you. We didn't know whether to come and look for you or call the police or what. Why on earth didn't you take your mobile?"

"I didn't think I'd be out for so long. I'm sorry." Eva sighed. "I hadn't expected to get caught up in the flow."

"The flow?" Her husband frowned at her. "The *flow*?"

She went to the dining room. There, at the table, sat her three children, each wearing a look of worry.

"Where were you, Mum?"

"I went for a walk."

"For five hours? How is that even possible?"

"It was easy. It didn't feel like five hours. The time flew by."

In the middle of the table sat a plate of toast, a tub of butter and a jar of jam.

"We made tea," Sadie said.

"It looks awesome," Eva replied.

"Well, *I* did the toast," Oscar said.

"But it was *my* idea to put the jam out," Sadie countered.

"Yeah, well, *I* did the butter. It would have been nothing without the butter." Summer tapped the butter tub with a long, lime green painted fingernail and raised her thickly pencilled eyebrows at them all.

"And *I've* made a pot of tea," Gavin placed the pot on the table.

"That's great," Eva said. "I'd love a cup of tea. Well done, everybody, you're all amazing."

She went and got the plates and knives out of the drawers, and a spoon for the jam, and some milk from the fridge, and mugs from the hooks, then sat down to eat. When she'd swallowed the last bite of her piece of toast, she got up, taking her plate to the sink.

"Where are you going?" Summer asked.

"Sorry, thanks for my tea," Eva replied. "I just really need a shower after that long walk." She looked at the empty toast plate in the middle of the table. "Great to see we've finally found a meal that we can all agree on, *and* it's vegetarian!"

She walked away from the table, feeling them all watching her. Guilt tugged: she didn't want to make them feel bad. After all, they had made tea. She turned back. "I really did enjoy my meal. Thank you, all of you."

"Well I guess this makes up for the Mother's Day you never had," Gavin said, a kind smile on his face.

"Yes, wonderful. Thanks."

"Will you go out for that long again, Mum?"

"Actually, I think I will. I mean, I think I'll go every day, now, for as long as I can."

"Well, that's good," Gavin said, the smile fading slightly, a wariness in his eyes. "But it would be better if you went earlier in the day, don't you think? So that you could get back -"

"Get back into the flow for longer?" Eva said. "Actually that's a great idea, Gav. Thanks!" She kissed his confused face, watching the certainty slipping away and the light of a mild panic appear in his eyes, pulling his eyebrows up. "I'll show you all where the salad drawer is, right after my shower, so you'll be equipped while I'm out."

She skipped up the stairs for her shower.

Wedding Day

I AM AN OLD WOMAN NOW, by anyone's standards. This August, should I live that long, I shall reach my one hundred and tenth birthday. My husband and friends have all passed away. I alone carry the memories of that spring, one hundred years ago, in the year 2020.

My family name was Philips, and a tradition evolved at some point in the early 1860s that the firstborn, assuming it would be a son – for it always had been – would be called Philip. There had been a Philip Philips for as long as anyone could remember; some poor fellow who spent his whole life explaining his ridiculous name to everyone he ever engaged with in any way beyond, "Hello".

I, however, remained a female baby, no matter how many times my father checked inside my nappy, and so was eventually named Philippa in a compromise that only served to illustrate the awful binding power of tradition failing to serve reality.

Ours was a small city, just twelve miles from the Kent Coast. Wealth and poverty tripped right over one another, but the two worlds rarely sat down to eat together. My family sat somewhere just outside the middle of the muddled pile, living as we did in the cemetery house.

The quaint Victorian building, formed in an L-shape, sat at the bottom of a hill which was covered in graves, their lines broken up here and there by vast elms and broad cedars. The hill stretched to the horizon, so that I imagined all the bodies in the ground lying as if on laid out on rising steps, from the bottom to the top.

I would play amongst the graves my father tended, and only had to hide when a new burial took place. Father dug new plots, and I would jump in and pretend I was trapped. I was always a clumsy child, and would often fall into the grave-holes by accident. One time, I really was unable to climb out. I began to panic, and my little arms and legs grew exhausted. It was my mother who found me, hauled me out by my wrists and beat me hard for my foolishness. After that, if he was in a good mood, Father would whistle me a signal in warning when Mother was out in the garden – which was not often.

Mother bought and sold things on Ebay, the internet auction site that celebrates its one hundred and thirty fifth birthday this year. It was a job that kept her mostly indoors on the computer. Both my parents' jobs continued pretty much as normal throughout the pandemic, with Mother benefitting from the closed high street, and Father digging twice as many graves as usual most weeks.

Our home, with its tombstone garden, stood slightly back from the main road into Canterbury. A few hundred yards from us lay the village of Sparkham, famous for its church tower and bell, which chimed every hour day and night. People who moved to Sparkham spent their first year learning how to sleep through the droning nightly gongs.

There was an old school, surrounded by some beautiful little Victorian cottages, a sprinkling of Tudor homes, and then an ugly 1960s housing estate. The estate's long gone now, while the Victorian cottages are standing as safe and solid as they were the day they were finished. I know, because I live in one now.

I went to Sparkham Primary School, and that was how I came to know Blaze Mitchell.

I wasn't drawn to him by any shared natural disposition. Indeed, he made me slightly afraid when I first knew him. Any time spent in his company was prone to end with some test of my character which I would invariably fail, never understanding why. He would laugh and shove me, his big mouth filling my view, his chipped teeth making me think of the gravestones in my garden.

Between my house at the cemetery and Blaze's home on the estate lay the newly built executive homes known as Great Sparkham Heights. The Developer's sign, its deep burgundy font edged with gold against a rich, cream background, boasted en-suite bedroom and luxury kitchen-diners. Most of the houses were finished and had families in, while the last few were in various stages of completion.

Often, after school, Blaze Cooper would walk behind me on my way home, calling me names as I went. I was a clumsy chunk of a child, and it made me a very easy target for Blaze.

During isolation, neither he nor I were supposed to be in school, because none of our parents were keyworkers. However, both his and my parents repeatedly sent us in to school in hopes that no one would realise, and they could be rid of us for the day. We were constantly being escorted back through the double doors and told to take ourselves back home again, since our parents refused to come and collect us.

One day as I was trudging home and Blaze was behind me, I found he was calling me to a game. It was a game we had played several times since the building of Sparkham Heights had begun, two years ago.

"Girl!" He called (he always called me 'Girl', even though he was the same age as me. How I hated him for it at the time!) "Girl! Come on, Girl, let's go down the Heights, come on!" Blaze never wanted to go home after school. I found out, years later, when life took Blaze and I on an unexpected journey together, that his own parents were not kind people. It explained most things about his childhood character.

I was afraid of the repercussions of saying no to Blaze, and so I mumbled my assent and followed him into the Sparkham Heights executive homes estate. The houses at the front were all finished, their perfect lawns squarely laid, their driveways neatly lined with shiny new cars, their lounges filled with corner sofas and gargantuan tellies. The pavements were wide and unused.

The building plots still in progress were at the back of the estate. There were rarely builders in evidence. Looking back now, I wonder if there must have been some sort of dispute or problem. We played for many months on two particular plots that didn't change or progress from foundations in one and a shell of breeze blocks in the other.

It was on our route to these plots that we saw the strange and tragic sight of Miss Saltmarsh in all her heart-breaking glory.

Hers was the fifth house into the estate. One of the grander ones, its double-fronted face had large windows and a veranda with a grey plastic-wicker sofa set on it. The grass was astro-turf perfect and the hanging baskets were show-home standard.

Everybody knew Miss Saltmarsh. At least, we knew her by title. She had been the Carnival Queen three years running. My own mother used to show me images of her online and ask if I'd like to be like Miss Saltmarsh one day. If I said yes, she'd tell me to keep away from the bread and jam; if I said no, she'd tell me it was just as well as I hadn't got a hope in hell of ever winning any kind of beauty contest.

Miss Saltmarsh had lived with her family, whose surname was Vashimah, until not long before. She had only recently bought this house in Sparkham Heights, fourteen miles away from the town of Saltmarsh and her parents. It had caused ripples and murmurs of disapproval, but Miss Saltmarsh did it anyway. I loved the sound of the word, Vashimah. I would whisper it over and over, until Mother slapped me, sharp and quick, in warning to be quiet. Miss Saltmarsh's actual first name, though, I don't recall. It may have been Nicole, but I can't be sure. I just remember her as Miss Saltmarsh Vashimah. She was exotic and glamorous, and she once came to our school to talk about all the charity work she did as part of her role as Miss Saltmarsh. She seemed like a film star to all us grubby, snot-smeared kids. She wouldn't let any of us touch her in the photos that were taken after assembly. She didn't like to be touched, she said to the photographer, who nodded once and then barked at us all to get away from her.

Her nails were long, pointed and painted thickly in baby blue. Her eyebrows were two dark, painted on stripes. False eyelashes made her eyes look as if they were deep in her head, peeking through fuzzy tunnels at us. She was the most fascinating collection of parts that I had ever seen.

Everyone in our corner of Kent knew who Miss Saltmarsh was, and not just because she got to ride on the biggest float at the annual carnival. Her other claim to fame, and the one that really impressed people far more than her beauty (which was mostly drawn on, sprayed on or stuck on), was the fact that she was engaged to a Premier League footballer.

From the moment they'd started seeing each other, shortly after they met at a glitzy charity gala event, Dean Cramp had been adopted as a new and beloved honorary Son of Saltmarsh. He and Miss Vashimah had been named as a local power couple, although nobody seemed clear about what their specific power was. We kids pictured them as if they were part of the New Avengers. All the boys were supposed to want to be him, and all us girls were supposed to want to be her.

The Vashimah's house had a name plate over the porch; Satish. All the other houses on the estate just had numbers. As we walked on our way to the building plots Blaze yanked at my hair, enjoying the way he could make my head jerk down to the right or left, depending on which side he pulled. I tried to shrug my shoulders up to my ears so that he couldn't get me, but his hard little bullet fingers were relentless and if he couldn't grab my hair he'd get hold of an ear lobe and yank on that instead. All the time he laughed his sneaky laugh, and I wished I could change schools or just go invisible and run around him unseen, perhaps pulling *his* ears, or, better still, pulling his school trousers down right there in the middle of Sparkham Heights.

So lost was I in these thoughts that it took me a while to realise that Blaze had stopped bothering me. We'd reached the part of the pavement that took us past the house named Satish. I looked at it, one eyebrow raised. I liked it more than the three story grim block of flats where Blaze lived, but not so much as my L-shaped cottage. My greatest impression was that it was wide and clean. There were no cars in the drive and it appeared deserted, until a sudden flash of white in the left hand bay window caught my eye. Blaze had seen it too; indeed, he'd seen it before me, and this flash of white was the merciful distraction that had dragged his hand from my hair.

"Come on!" He hissed his order and I followed him without question across the perfect bright lawn to the steps of the veranda. Up we slipped, backs bent low, heads down, eyes up. We ran silent and stealthy, following the walls of the house, until we came to the end of the veranda, which stopped by way of a wooden rail just short of the feature bay window. Blaze turned to me, his eyes alive with all sorts of unspoken thrills, and raised a trembling finger to his lips. I nodded, and together, we peeked over the wooden railing and through the angled side of the bay window.

Inside was the strangest sight I had ever seen. I knew it was wrong to spy, and crouching there, next to the hated Blaze, I was uncomfortable and more than a little afraid.

Miss Saltmarsh stood before a fine mirror, pouting at her own reflection. But it was the dress that had caught our attention. It was a luminescent white, brighter than white, even. A shining mix of satin and silk, with lace detailing and a veil that hung down from her hair, dotted with pearls and sequins that caught the light and reflected a thousand rainbows on the ceiling and walls of the room. She was swaying in time to some music we could not hear from our place on the veranda. Her dark, sleek hair was pulled back tightly from her smooth, orange forehead, and laced with more pearls. Her cheeks were highlighted and bronzed, giving her the contoured appearance of a robot, as was the fashion with some girls back then. Her eyelashes were thick and deep as birds' nests or moustaches. Her lips were peach and her top lip glistened with sweat, which may well have resulted from the wrestling match that Miss Saltmarsh must have gone through to get her body into that dress.

"She's gone all fat!" Blaze whispered, his eyes feasting on her gloriously rounded form.

It was true: isolation seemed to have drastically altered her body shape.

"Lucky for her the carnival's cancelled," Blaze laughed.

"I like her like that," I said. "She looks like maybe she wouldn't get cross if you touched her now."

But her dress wouldn't quite do up at the back, and ripe, round skin overflowed around the arm sockets. Clearly when she'd been measured up for it, she'd been a good deal smaller.

Blaze had begun to giggle somewhere in the back of his throat, a sound that was like the empty click of a toy gun trigger being pulled fast, repeatedly. "What are you laughing at?" I frowned, still taking in the scene. The room was filled with white roses. There were vases of them on the table, the mantelpiece and the floor. In the middle of the table was a towering cake, one round sponge placed atop another, getting smaller and smaller as they rose, with just the lightest scrape of icing around them. On the shelf created by each layer were draped redcurrants and scattered blueberries, raspberries and strawberries.

"She's got the same cake as Harry and Meghan had," I said. (They were the royal couple who had married a year or two before. They were hot news at the time and my mother had been obsessed with them, and had made money by buying and selling service sheets from the wedding through EBay. Of course, no one remembers them now, but that's another story.)

"Who are you, the Royal Correspondent?" Blaze shoved me hard. I fell, teeth first, into a bar of the railings and yelped in pain. "Shut up!" came Blaze's panicked warning, but it was too late: I'd given us away. Miss Saltmarsh's face appeared at the window. "Run!" Blaze screamed, as he turned and fled. I tried to follow but tripped on my own feet and fell, flat out on the deck of the veranda. The hard ridges pressed into my fleshy knees. I looked ahead of me and saw one perfect white stiletto and one strangely bare foot, its toenails thickly coated in baby blue varnish. I was so close I could see the fair hairs sprouting on those otherwise childishly podgy toes.

I followed the line of the toes along the foot, to a pair of puffy ankles which disappeared under the radiant lacy hem of the most beautiful dress I had ever seen.

Miss Saltmarsh Vashimah stood over me, hands on hips, one thick eyebrow raised in question, and the question was, undoubtedly, *what are you doing on my veranda?*

I could only stare.

"Ain't you scared of me?" She said, with a weird smile that had a sort of boast to it. "Do you know who I am?"

"I do."

"And do you know what today should have been?" She raised the second eyebrow to meet the first.

"I'm going to take a wild guess that it's your wedding day," I said.

"You've got it," she smiled, and reached down a hand. I stayed where I was, as flat as could be against the decking. "Well, come on," she said, "Get up!" Still I remained prostrate.

"We're not supposed to be this close together," I said.

"Oh. Yeah. You're right." She stepped back, away from me. "*You* might have *it*."

I pushed myself onto all fours, then slowly got to my feet, keeping my eyes on her all the time. "I haven't got it," I said.

She didn't care. "Do you know what this disease has done to me?"

I was on the verge of saying, "It's made you eat too much," when she touched her hand to the left side of her chest.

"It's broken my heart," she said, and as she blinked, a large tear began its slow journey from its eye to the tip of her lashes. "Today I should be at Saltmarsh, getting married on the beach, surrounded by the local and national press. Hello magazine were due to come *here*, to Satish, next month to take pictures of us living our dreams. We were gonna be a six page spread. Right at this moment I should be staring into Dean's eyes and making my vows. My life was gonna begin today… Instead… Instead I ain't seen Dean in two months and no one's taking any pictures of anyone unless they're in full PPE and working in the NHS coz there's only one story in the whole world right now and it isn't *me*!" she sobbed, and spit flew from those lips that bulged like over-inflated bicycle inner tyres. "I'm tired," she said. "I'm tired and I've finished watching Tiger King and I've drunk so much tea even the thought of it gives me a headache. I needed a diversion. I couldn't get my money back on the flowers or the cake, so I thought, stuff it! I'll have 'em all! At least my house will smell nice and I won't have to cook."

By now, a row of tears was caught in her eyelashes, like dew drops on black grass. My heart ached for her. She'd had it all – and now, thanks to that damned virus – it had been yanked from her fists. An idea formed in my mind.

"I know a place you could go where everyone will watch you," I said.

She stopped crying. "You do?" she said.

"I know two, actually," I said, thinking fast. "Double the crowds."

"Really? I didn't think there was anywhere like that left," she said.

"Follow me," I said.

"Hang on," she disappeared back inside Satish. When she came out she had both shoes on and carried two bouquets of flowers, one of which she gave to me. "You can be my bridesmaid," she said. We set off together, down the road towards the school. What a strange, groom-less bridal party we made: a scruffy flower-girl in school uniform and a beauty queen in all her finery. People began to come out from their homes to take photographs on their phones.

"Oh my God, girl," she said to me, "This is gonna go viral. I'm gonna go viral!" She laughed with wild joy and punched the air with her bouquet.

When we got to school, the children rushed to crowd around, but the teachers held them all back at a two metre distance, which Miss Saltmarsh looked relieved at.

"There is *one* good thing about Corona," she said, standing there waving at the children from an invisible island in the playground.

"You look like a princess!" the little girls shouted, while the boys tried to out-do one another in volume. "Marry me!" "Marry *me*!" "Not *him*, me!" Miss Saltmarsh stood there, smiling beatifically at them all, glowing like a religious vision, receiving their worship like an empty jug being filled.

As we processed to the graveyard, a line of spectators followed, a safe distance between each one. My mother saw us coming and rushed out to meet us. She hit me hard around the side of my head and asked me what the hell I thought I was doing. Miss Saltmarsh explained everything to her.

"What are you going to do with all your cake?" My mother asked, strangely interested.

"Dunno," came the reply.

"Well don't eat it. You've already piled on enough since you've been locked away. Just look at the state of you!"

Miss Saltmarsh looked crestfallen. I burned with shame at my Mother's sharp tongue.

"I can get your money back on your cake," Mother said. A light seemed to go on in Miss Saltmarsh's eyes.

"You can? How?"

"EBay. No problem. You drop your cake to me and I'll have the cash in your account by this time tomorrow."

I watched Miss Saltmarsh think it over for a few seconds. "Done!" she announced. "I'll be back with the cake."

She turned and looked at all the people watching. They lined the road in the same way people do when the Olympic torch passes by. Miss Saltmarsh walked through them, down the middle of the road, nodding graciously at the crowds as she went.

My mother smacked me around the other side of my head and sent me indoors, yanking the bouquet from my hands as I passed. I found it, later, laid upon an old mossy grave marked Gargery: a distant relative on my Mother's side.

She sold the cake quickly. Every last slice of it. And the story of the cake sale and the wedding procession made the news. Many were furious because they said we'd broken the self-isolation rules, but Miss Saltmarsh was thrilled. She wrote a card to me, thanking me for the part I had played in her magical day. She said I was better than the bridesmaids she was supposed to have had.

And, best of all, Blaze stopped picking on me from that day on. I suppose he was ashamed and cross with himself because he'd run away so fast and lost his part in the drama. Now, people respected me. They asked me again and again to tell my story, while Blaze sulked and sloped off.

At first, I enjoyed watching his discomfort, but my nature doesn't seem able to hold onto a grudge. One day, I sought him out. He was sitting alone, on a bench near our school. Not allowed in, not wanted at home. Just like me.

"Let's be friends," I held my hand out.

"We have always been friends," he said, taking my hand and rising. Our eyes met and he smiled. There was no meanness now, only a faint light of mischief and hope. "Is it true that you get to play in the fresh grave-holes?" he asked.

I smiled. "I do." I beckoned him with one finger, giggling as I did so. "Come on. Follow me."

We walked together towards the graveyard, and so began a new era for me and for Blaze in that last year of primary school during an unprecedented time of national crisis. A new course was being set: an understanding of family circumstance through shared experience; a love that grew and lasted all the way into a new century.

I did not know it at that moment, but, quite silently, as we crept and hid and spied between the graves, the midday sun warming our faces and the seagulls high above us crying for bread, love crept in, and there was never so much as even a shadow of another parting from him.

CATTICUS AND MAUDIE

MAUDIE STOOD AT HER FRONT DOOR STEP, both hands gripping the rubber handle on her tartan shopping trolley, grunting with the effort of bumping it up and over her doorstep.

"You'd be better off pulling," Ray called over the low wall that, thankfully, divided their homes.

"Mm," Maudie acknowledged, lips tightly pursed, too breathless to speak. Just pulling the trolley back from Aldi had been hard enough. The whole morning had felt like a horrible test.

"I'd help but I can't come near you," Ray whined.

"No, don't come near," Maudie said quickly, holding a hand out to keep Ray away. Social distancing had been a relief, where Ray was concerned. What she could do with was a ban on talking at all, just for him. Once Ray got talking, he could go for hours, and he wasn't interested in a word anyone else had to say. She wondered for a moment if she could write to Boris Johnson and get him to do some sort of announcement specifically to catch Ray: "Ray Gorgonbow of Crowborough Road, please refrain from talking to your neighbour as of now. This ban is to be held for the rest of your life, regardless of when the Covid-19 crisis is over." She smiled faintly at the thought.

"What you need is to get a purchase on the threshold with one foot. Place the other behind you, as if you're doing a squat."

"A what?"

"Squat."

What was he talking about now? From her new position, pulling the trolley from inside the doorway, her face out of Ray's eye-line, she rolled her eyes. Then, discovering the pleasure in it, she poked her tongue out at him. He wittered on, oblivious to everything but the sound of himself.

"I might be old but I'm not an idiot," Maudie muttered, pulling the trolley hard. It suddenly gave a lurch and was in her hallway so fast that she nearly fell backwards.

"There you go," an unknown young woman stood on her doorstep, beaming at her. "All in."

Maudie stared back in horror. "Are you two metres away? Please keep two metres away," was all she could say.

"Yeah, yeah, relax!" the girl said, laughing and swatting Maudie's concerns away with a flap of her hand. "Listen, I just did you a favour, yeah? I pushed your trolley in, yeah?"

"Thank you," Maudie shut her door, a view of the girl's offended expression the last thing she saw before sealing herself in. She heard the girl exclaim, and swear, and then laugh; then Ray began speaking to her, poor thing. Maudie didn't want to hear any of this. She just wanted to be inside and safe. Boris had said today that everyone over seventy must self-isolate. At eighty-three, with osteoporosis and a heart murmur, Maudie couldn't lock herself in fast enough.

The trolley was filled with enough tins to get her through three weeks at least, and plenty of long-life milk. She'd got eggs and jam and crumpets. All the other bread had been raided, but crumpets suited Maudie just fine. She took them out of the large packets and separated them into pairs in sandwich bags, then laid them neatly in the freezer.

The tins went into the pantry cupboard. As she stood there, she saw in the back of the cupboard the can of Whiskas that had been there for the last year, untouched. She still couldn't bear to get rid of it. But, oh, how she wished Catticus were here, right now!

He'd been a gorgeous ginger tom, thick-legged and fat-tailed, always in a good mood and always eager for gentle human contact. He'd come to her unexpectedly from neighbours down the road, who had emigrated to New Zealand. They'd knocked on the door one night, and asked if she would take him.

With Alf, her husband, being only six months gone, she was feeling an emptiness in the house. Their children had left home, one to Scotland and the other to Cornwall, neither of them married or even settled with anyone they'd introduced her to, and time ticking on as it can't help but do. Now Maudie sat, like a pin on a vast map, a mere dot to show the lonesome point precisely between her offspring. Catticus couldn't have come at a better time.

Maudie had always had cats as a girl. The few photos that remained from her childhood always had one, somewhere in the frame, usually draped across her body somehow. But Alf had been allergic and severely asthmatic, so there was no possibility of furry pets.

She stacked the tinned curry and soup into the cupboard, thinking only of Catticus and how much she missed him. She could hardly bear to admit it, but she felt his absence more than she felt Alf's these days.

At first she didn't consciously register the feeling of pressure against her leg, accepting it as part of the depth of her memory, recalling the very way Catticus used to push himself against her legs, weaving figure-eights around and around her ankles.

Instinctively, she leaned down to one side to stroke the cat she felt so warming and weightily against her. But when she placed her hand where his old back should be, there was nothing there.

She looked down sharply.

"Catticus?" she called.

No mew returned her question. She shut the cupboard door and shuffled off to check the rest of downstairs: another cat must have ventured in through the cat flap, for there was no question that a cat had, indeed, just rubbed up against her. But there was no sign of a cat anywhere.

"Maudie, Maudie, Maudie," she said with a weary smile and a shrug. "I think this is what they call a Senior Moment."

The shopping all put neatly away, Maudie made a pot of tea. She set a tray with a cup and saucer, and a dainty jug of milk. She placed two rich tea biscuits from the barrel onto a pretty blue plate, and set the pot beside it, then carried the tray through to the front room where she placed it on the largest of her nest of tables. She settled into her green velour sofa, and reached for the radio that sat on another side table, next to the arm of the sofa. She was just in time to hear the morning's play.

Beside her on the sofa lay a wicker basket, filled with softly coloured wools and crochet hooks. She picked up the project she had been working on – a dress for a friend's first great-grandchild - and settled down to it. But a sudden prod on her lap made her drop the wool.

There was nothing there. And yet, she felt it again: the push, as of two fat paws, down against her thigh. It was unmistakable, and wonderfully familiar.

"Catticus?"

The weight on her legs moved and – there was no doubt about it – circled on her lap. Then it paused, all movement ceased, yet she still felt four points of solid pressure on her legs.

Maudie sat, crochet hook held aloft, mouth open, staring at her empty lap.

"Am I losing my marbles?" she asked her knees. As if in response, there was a sudden heavy feeling, just as there used to be when Catticus finally settled in her lap to rest, and let his full body weight fall against hers.

"Catticus?"

There was no sound, but as Maudie breathed in deeply, she sensed the faintest whiff of a familiar smell.

"Catticus?"

She leaned forward for the teapot, and as she did, she felt his shape, solid against the crease of her belly. How could this be? She poured her tea, and sat back.

"Catticus," she said, and felt the unmistakable rub of his head against her wrist. She cupped her hand around the air where his head would have been, and made a tickling motion with her fingers.

"You've come to keep me company, have you? While I'm all alone."

The cat's form kept close to Maudie all day, and later, when she settled herself into bed, she felt his weight by her feet.

"Goodnight, Catticus," she smiled, and turned off the light. "You'll stay with me through all of this, won't you, dear?"

And Catticus did.

OPENING

DEAR ISAAC,

I know it's hard right now. I know your body's going through all sorts of changes and your emotions are probably all over the place etc. Remember, I <u>have been</u> a teenager, <u>I know what it's like</u>. I guess we've hit a patch where it would be really useful to have your Dad around, I suppose. Perhaps you'd talk to him. Certainly you don't seem to want to say anything to me. It's been a week since you last grunted in my direction. You shut yourself away in your room. You won't eat with me anymore.

We used to be so close. When you were little, there was nothing we couldn't talk about. And now, suddenly, you're just... gone. I'm the same as I ever was. I'm your Mum. I deserve some respect. Why don't you respect me? I suppose you'd respect your father, if he were here.

I know this disease is scary. Are you scared? Because I'm scared. You're so absorbed in your own feelings you don't stop to consider mine, do you? I'm terrified, Isaac. I spend all day worrying about Grandma. She keeps going out! And she won't listen to anything I say. I guess that must run in the family. But while we're in this lockdown, you could at least make some effort to communicate. We're the only company each other have.

I'm slipping this note under your door because I can't think how else to communicate with you. You won't talk to me. You ignore my texts. You switch off your phone when I call it. Don't pretend you don't, I <u>know</u> that you do. I hear it get turned off because I'm standing <u>outside your bedroom door!!</u>

My last hope is that you'll read this. I have a terrible feeling that you may just throw it in the bin.

But if you want to write back, you can.

Love, Mum

Dear Mum,

Leave me alone.

Isaac.

Dear Isaac,

You'll never understand how your 'letter' made me feel until you have kids of your own. If you ever do. I mean, I find it hard to imagine that you'll ever form a relationship and get to the stage of having children with the way you behave at the moment, but I suppose it could happen. One day. Anyway, your words cut me like a knife.

I carried you in my body for nine months!! I sat and nursed you, and taught you to walk and talk and ride a bike, to write your name… I've poured my life out <u>for you</u> all these years. Fifteen years I've been basically bleeding out <u>for you</u>!! I've put all my desires on the back burner. I've sacrificed everything to do my best <u>for you</u>. And I had to keep going all by myself when your father walked out.

Son, we've been in lockdown for a week now. Just you and me in this flat. And you haven't spoken a single word to me. I can't go on like this. You need to start talking.

Love, Mum

Dear Mum,

I'm sorry I ruined your life. I didn't ask to be born.

Isaac.

Dear Isaac,

Of course you didn't ruin my life. <u>Of course you didn't!!</u> You have made my life <u>worthwhile</u>!! I was glad to give things up for you because you were better than all the things I gave up!!

Of course I realise you didn't ask to be born. I get that. We all feel like that from time to time. But I'm glad you were born despite everything. I <u>am</u>!! I wish you'd show a little gratitude for the life you have, is all!! I've done my bit for you. It's been so hard at times because I've had to do it all on my own but I've always tried my best.

Love, Mum

Dear Mum,

If it's gratitude you're after, well thank you very much.

Thank you for bringing me into a dying world, where you'll be long gone and I'll be left to burn to death with the rest of my generation. Or drown under the melting polar ice caps and rising sea levels. Thanks for that.

Isaac.

Dear Isaac,

<u>None</u> of that is <u>my</u> fault!!

Love, Mum

Dear Mum,

It's your generation that wrecked the earth and, as I can't speak to them all at once, you are their representative. So, as a representative of the current generation, I'm telling you, your generation <u>sucks</u>.

And let's not even get started on Brexit. Or how I'll never be able to afford a house of my own. Or college. Thanks a bunch.

Isaac.

Dear Isaac,

Ok, I get it, I get it. You're right. Do you hear me? I'm saying <u>you're right!!</u> Your generation is facing unique challenges. But Greta Thomberg doesn't lie in bed watching YouTube all day long, does she? She's probably planting a tree somewhere <u>right now!!</u>

I'm going to jog on the spot on the balcony every night from 7 until 7.30. If you want to run with me, meet me there.

Love, Mum

P.S. Anyway, if you're so worried about the planet, how come I'm the only one in this house who bothers to recycle?

Dear Isaac,

Ok. It's been two days.

I guess I hit a nerve.

Thank you for sorting out the recycling pile. Yes, I noticed. And, yes, I appreciate it. I'd love to thank you in person sometime.

So… what's this new silence about? Are you sulking with me? Did I take away your moral high ground and ruin your fun?

Come on, Isaac! We're locked up here together! With no one else to talk to! Couldn't you do with a little conversation? I'm sure you could. I think it would do <u>you good</u>.

You ought to come out and talk to me for the sake of your <u>own mental health</u>.

Oh, I know your generation think they invented mental health but, guess what? It was actually <u>my</u> generation who invented that! All your self-help and be-nice business started thanks to us Irresponsible Old Farts, so there you go. We may have burned up the atmosphere but at least we gave you the tools to explore how you feel about that. You'll thank me for that one day, when you've stopped sulking.

Love, Mum

Dear Isaac,

Please, please, won't you <u>just write to me</u>? You must have <u>something</u> to say?

Love, Mum

Dear Isaac,

I'm sorry. I think I might have gone a bit bonkers, perhaps. Sorry, Isaac.

I was sorting through a box last night and I came across an old diary I kept when I was fifteen. It was... helpful.

Anyway, look. I know this is all so weird. I appreciate that it must be very hard to have no structure to your day. That there must feel as if there's no point in getting out of bed.

I'm trying to guess at how you feel – but I probably should just ask.

How are you feeling? I really do care about how you feel, and I really do want to know. I love you. How are you?

Love, Mum x

Dear Mum,

I'm ok, I guess. I wasn't sulking, I'm just hanging out here, passing the time.

I remember when I was a kid, and in the summer holidays we'd bake fairy cakes and biscuits, and you'd get the play-doh out, and I'd dig beside you in the garden. I've been lying here thinking about it. It was nice. I remember you used to let me paint my fingernails with your nail polish, and one time Grandpa saw me with bright red finger and toe nails and he freaked out... Do you remember that?

Those were good days, Mum. I see that. But I was a little kid. I'm just not a kid anymore. And this isn't a long summer holiday. It's my life, it's my school time. I can't hang out with the people who make me feel like... like the me I am now. I'm different at school than I am at home. I mean, I'm still me, but I'm also... I'm sort of someone you don't know. Not in a bad way.

I get it that you're stressing out. Have you tried calling Auntie Phoebe? Why don't you call her for a chat? You always say you don't speak to her enough. It might do you good.

Isaac

Dear Isaac,

The maturity of your letter has blown me away, son!! I can see that you are someone I don't know!! I saw it there on the page.

Who are you? What do you like to read, to watch, to listen to? Who do you admire? What do you think about all this Corona business?

Love, Mum xx

Dear Mum,

Well, I'm not a whole new person, you know. I'm still Isaac who hates the spoon put into his porridge and who can't tie his laces in under five minutes and who loves

Nutella on pancakes. That's still me. It's just that, you're the only one who knows that's still me these days.

I don't really read anything. But I like watching movies. But you wouldn't like any of the movies I watch. And I watch a lot of YouTube. Mostly short films people have made. I'd like to study that one day. I've been making little stop motion animations in my bedroom. Perhaps I'll show you one. I sometimes post them online. People seem to like them.

I hate Corona for what it's taken away from me. But I'm glad the planet is getting a chance to heal a bit. Except I read online that if everyone goes back to normal after this, all the environmental good will be undone anyway.

Do you think things ever will go back to normal? I think that is my fear. That nothing will ever go back to the way it was. That this is how it'll be forever, now. I mean, they still don't have a vaccine for SARS, do they? So there's no guarantee. I guess I feel like this might be the apocalypse.

Isaac

P.S. I'm sorry to tell you this, but mental health as a phenomenon existed way before your generation discovered they could make money out of it.

Dear Isaac,

I love you.

I don't know when things will go back to normal.

I don't know how to fix all the things that are already wrong.

I don't even know what stop motion animation is. But I want to know.

I love you so much. I'm sorry for every time I've blown it with you. I never meant to. I just love you.

Love, Mum xxx

Dear Mum,

I know. I love you too.

If you want, I'll show you one of my movies later. Meet me in the kitchen at 9pm?

Love, Isaac x

KEEPING UP

"IF ONLY WE'D HAD MORE CHILDREN," Rowena said, emptying the dishwasher for what felt like the fifteenth time today.

At the kitchen table, trying to concentrate on the laptop screen, Darren's eyebrow flicked up and down in response. The laptop he'd brought home from work was raised up on top of an upturned cardboard box to make it ergonomically good, if aesthetically bad. "Really?" he said.

"Yes. Really."

The two offspring of Rowena and Darren Bond were still asleep, it being only 11am. Their youngest was due to wake in about half an hour, but the eldest had proven to possess a talent for lying in bed until well into the afternoon.

"Why on earth would you want more?" Darren's fingers flew over the keyboard. His speed typing was one of the things that had attracted Rowena to him when they'd first met, both working in the same office, twenty years ago. ("You play that thing like Mozart" she remembered saying to him about his keyboard skills back then, and cringed.)

"If we'd had more, we might have had some who actually *did* something, you know?"

Darren stopped typing and turned to look his wife full in the face. "Or it might mean that we had four or five children lying in bed right now, instead of just two."

"You know the Martins down the road?" Rowena ignored him.

She shut the dishwasher door and turned the kettle on to boil for what might well have been the sixty-fifth time that day, then gave up waiting for his response to her question. "Well, anyway, their youngest has built a family website."

That got his attention.

"What? Isn't he, like, eight or something?"

"That's right! He's built a website and the whole family are blogging, taking it in turns to write a diary every day, so that at the end of all this, they'll have a detailed family record of life in confinement."

Darren smirked. "I think Anne Frank beat them to that."

"I'm serious Darren. And I heard yesterday that a publisher has picked it up and it's going to be in the book shops and on the supermarket shelves when all this is over and it'll be sure to be a bestseller and so their kid will have paid their mortgage off before he's finished primary school!"

Darren sat back, slumped in his chair. "That *is* annoying," he admitted.

"And Gus and Karen's kids have set up a home gym made from things they've found and recycled and they're doing circuits every day, altogether, and they're having a *great* time."

"Ours might do something like that."

"Oh yeah, sure, if they'd get off their backsides and someone took them to the shed and showed them all the stuff and built it for them and did the exercise in their place."

"Yes, that's a more likely scenario," Darren had to agree. His fingers returned to the keys.

"And Sheena's boy has set up a band via Zoom. They're doing a live concert on YouTube this week. And Martha's girls have created a model village and set the houses out along their road and apparently it's become a local tourist attraction for everyone on their daily walks. And they've put lighting circuits in each one that are solar powered and switch on automatically at sundown. And Matthew and Ellie's boys picked up a language each to learn and Emma's kids took over the cooking so that she hasn't made dinner for three weeks now and Brian's two have written a play they're going to perform in their front garden for neighbours to watch and make donations to the NHS for. I mean, I could go on, Darren."

"I have a feeling you will," he said.

"The only person who makes me feel better is Felicity McGregor, whose kids seem even worse than ours. They fight each other all day and they're not lifting a finger to help her. She's exhausted. And, of course, Ted's off isolating with that awful other woman so she's all alone. She keeps asking people to make meals for her, and three of her friends have ordered takeaways for her in the last week out of pity. I think Terry Butler is even trying to get her a trampoline so that those mad boys of hers can bounce some energy off."

"He's always had a soft spot for Felicity."

Rowena placed a mug of tea in front of Darren on the table and took a good swig from her own. Darren stopped typing to drink with her.

"How do you know all this stuff, anyway?" he asked.

"Facebook."

"Ugh. *Fake*book," he said, pulling a face.

"I mean, it's as much as our two can manage to do to get out of bed. Dylan hasn't changed his clothes for four days and Izzie probably has no idea what day it is. They say they get their school work done but, honestly, they do not do a scrap more than is absolutely necessary. And meanwhile, everyone around them is building their skillset and they'll be left behind. I can't bear it, Darren. It's driving me crazy!"

Darren leaned back in his chair, mug in hand and smiled. "You know, there's a simple solution to all this," he said, glad to have solved his wife's problem so easily.

"Which is?"

"Stop looking at Facebook." He took a long, deep slurp of tea and went back to his typing.

"Oh, no, I can't come off of Facebook," Rowena put her tea down hard to emphasise her point.

"Why ever not?"

"I'd miss Felicity McGregor too much."

A Matter of Time

"I LOVE YOU SO MUCH," Frank's sweet voice whispered into the answerphone. Ella had let the machine pick it up for the express purpose of being able to listen to Frank on repeat. The soft, secret tones sent little pin-pricks of pleasure up and down her body, from her ankles to her crown.

She played the message again and again over the next few hours of her solitary afternoon. The spreadsheets she was supposed to be working on in preparation for a Zoom meeting the next morning were attempted in a half-hearted way, and abandoned. There was no hope of focusing on spreadsheets while Frank had a voice and said things like that.

He texted her, too. *I can't bear the thought that it might be weeks before we get 2 C each other*, he wrote. *There must b sum way we can meet.* And then, later, *But I don't think I could bare 2 C U & not touch U!*

Was he The One? Maybe. The 2s and the Cs and the Us of his text were pushed aside in favour of the sentiment. In focussing thus, Frank became her one, True Knight, and Ella, Rapunzel, with the global pandemic cast as wicked stepmother, shutting them both away in their towers.

They had only met twice, the day before lockdown had begun. Ella was helping a friend buy a house, and had gone with her to a viewing: a viewing facilitated by Frank. Her friend was still in two minds over the property, but Ella's mind was clear about Frank: he was gorgeous. And, while her friend had failed to make an offer as yet, Frank had wasted no time in making an offer of his own to Ella. They'd spent that evening in a pub, and Ella had dared to hope that, this time, she'd finally struck gold.

When the Zoom meeting began the next morning, Ella texted her colleagues to say her internet was down and she needed to reschedule. For the rest of the day, she tried to focus and get some of the figures on the spreadsheet sorted. It was hard to concentrate, though, with Frank's constant missives, which grew more passionate by the hour.

Frank had been furloughed now, which he said he was glad of anyway. He didn't really want to be an estate agent. He wanted to be a musician, he was *born* to be a musician, really, but there was no money in it unless you were Elton John, Frank said. Poor Frank! Ella's heart ached for him and the career he should be having.

I'm gonna write a song about U 1 of these days. He often texted Ella to say. The thought of the song kept her awake at night, tingling with the romantic thrill of it all. She had never met an actual musician before she'd met Frank. She hadn't heard him sing yet, but she could tell from the way he spoke of his reverence for his craft that he was as talented as he believed himself to be. He was right, she was sure: it was only a matter of time.

And then Boris made the announcement that changed things at last.

We may not be able to meet up, Frank's text popped up within seconds of the news, *but it turns out I can employ you as my cleaner! How does £5 p.hr sound? Wear a sexy French maid's outfit and get UR sexy self over here asap!*

Ella giggled at the message and changed her tracksuit bottoms for her favourite pair of jeans.

When she got to Frank's place, he was waiting at the door for her. Her heart seemed to somersault in her chest at the sight of him. The way his hair fell over his eyes, his blue jeans and white T-shirt all looked even more handsome than she remembered.

"Hi," she smiled, leaning towards him for a kiss. He jumped back as if she'd tried to bite him.

"Not out here! There are people snitching on people, you know? Calling the police and stuff. You should have come with a broom or something. Something to make you look like a cleaner."

Ella looked nervously up and down the street. There was no sign of anyone.

"Hang on," Frank said, and disappeared inside. He reappeared moments later with a mop.

"What's that for?"

"Just so you look the part," Frank chuckled.

"Oh, right!" Ella returned his laugh. "All part of the fun, I suppose," she said.

Frank stepped back into the hallway. "Come in, then," he said.

"Who's there, Frankie-boy?" a voice called from the living room.

"It's that cleaner I told you about," Frank smiled widely and winked at Ella. "Just a bit of fun," he whispered. "Didn't think they'd react too well if they knew I was having my girlfriend round when neither of them has seen theirs." He tapped the side of his nose.

Ella nodded and blinked, adjusting to the darkness of the dirty cream-grey hallway after the glaring sun outside. A great stack of recycling spilled over the top of a plastic bin, and bikes leaned against every other available bit of wall space. She followed Frank, walking sideways to avoid pedals, handlebars and oily bike-chains, through to the characterless, cold lounge. Cigarette smoke hung suspended like a layer of cloud over the heads of Frank's housemates, who slumped on the sagging leather sofa, both dressed in pyjamas and playing a fighting game on the Xbox.

"So… this is where you live." Ella took in the bland, colourless décor and grimy carpet. "Still, I suppose your room's nice?"

"You'd like to start in my room?" Frank said, speaking in a false, over-loud way for the others to hear and winking as if he were on a stage at Christmas. "Sure, I'll show you the way. Just showing the cleaner where our rooms are, boys," he said to his housemates, who grunted in reply.

Up in Frank's room they were able to drop the pretence.

"My darling," he said, wrapping his arms around her. "Forgive me. It's just that we've gotta make this convincing for Craig and Grant. It's gotta seem like you really *are* a cleaner."

"But why?"

"Because Grant works for the police and Craig's a civil servant. If it came out that they'd broken lockdown rules there could be serious consequences for both of them. They could lose their jobs."

"Oh," Ella said. "Perhaps I should go, then?"

"No, no, no need for that! We're alone, at last." Frank ran his fingers through her hair. He leaned in to kiss her.

"You look even better than I remember," he breathed. She smiled.

"So do you," she said, letting his hands wander deliciously up and down her back.

Then, without warning, Frank threw her from him violently and jumped across the room to his doorway as if a bolt of electricity had shot through him. His housemate was standing there, wanting to know if Frank had taken the last Muller Light yogurt from the fridge.

While his housemate talked yogurt, Frank explained, in far too many words, that the cleaner was just tidying his room. He gave Ella a look that was easily interpreted as, *DO IT!* so she busied herself tidying clothes from the floor into piles, stifling the urge to giggle as she separated out the dirty laundry and neatening the magazines strewn about the room. Frank disappeared with his housemate, returning moments later with a vacuum cleaner.

"We'd better at least make it look genuine," he said. He handed Ella the vacuum. "The plug's down there," he pointed to the floor behind the bed. "I'll pop downstairs, just to make it look right," he said, and disappeared.

Ella stood for a moment or two, unsure how to proceed. Frank returned, as if he sensed her hesitation. He pointed at the vacuum. "You'd better turn it on," he said, "Or they might get suspicious." And with that, he disappeared downstairs.

Ella vacuumed the three bedrooms and then the flight of stairs down to the lounge. Frank nodded enthusiastic encouragement at her, and she understood this as her cue to vacuum the lounge, too.

"Lift your feet," she said to Craig and Grant, recalling how her mother used to say that to her and her brother on Saturday mornings while they were watching telly.

"Is she doing the kitchen and toilet, too?" One of Frank's housemates asked, eyes fixed on the screen, thumb flicking frantically on his controller.

"Obviously. I mean, she's a real cleaner. And, of course, that's what real cleaners do, isn't it?" Frank avoided Ella's glare, but she knew he felt it. Finally, he turned to face her, and she was relieved to see that shame had painted a flush on his cheeks. "I'm sorry, I can't offer you a cup of tea," he said.

"Oh, it's alright, I trust you don't have any germs," Ella replied. "You told me it was safe to come. I'd actually love one."

"It's not that. There's no mugs. They're all piled up in the sink. But, perhaps when you do the kitchen, you could make yourself one. You'd just have to wash the cup up first."

At that, Ella dropped the vacuum cleaner and began to walk away. Frank jumped up and into her path.

"Hey!" he said, lowering his face so that their eyes met. "Come on!"

"Yeah," Craig or Grant joined in, not moving their face from the screen. "You're being paid to clean, man, so *clean*!"

Ella stared in disbelief. Frank held his palms out and shrugged at his housemate's words.

"Let me show you the kitchen," he said, trying to convey some sort of significant look by widening his eyes at her. Ella followed him. Once they were both standing on the lino, he shut the door between them and his housemates and grabbed her shoulders.

"God, I'm so sorry! I'm so sorry, my darling, this is dreadful for both of us!"

"Although mostly for me," Ella said.

"Do you have any idea what hell it is to see you and not be able to take you in my arms and kiss you? Not to be able to introduce you as my girlfriend? It's hell!"

"So why don't you just drop the pretence and do those things?"

"Their jobs, Ella, their *careers*!"

"Oh, yeah, you said."

He looked directly into her eyes, holding her gaze, moving his head with hers when she tried to look away.

"Look, I know this hasn't gone quite to plan –"

"You're telling me!"

"But we're still *together*, aren't we? We're still in the same room at last." He pulled her close. "I've missed you so much." She let him hold her, without responding. Finally, he whispered into her hair. "Look, I think for the sake of appearances, it would be better if you just do the kitchen."

She moved away, opened her mouth to protest, but he carried on.

"Don't worry about the bathroom, we can do that. Hey, in fact, I'll do it myself – how's that sound? And I'll even tell the boys *you* did it. What about that, then?"

She stared at his beautiful face with his high cheek bones, dark eyes and neatly trimmed beard. He was the best looking boyfriend she had ever had, there was no doubt about it. His hands felt good on her waist. His mouth began to pull up into a smile... she couldn't resist the look in his eyes.

"Okay," she heard herself say, knowing that later she would hate herself for saying it. "Okay."

"Right," he stepped backwards. "I'd better go back to the lounge. You know, act normal and all that." He nodded as he passed her on his way out of the kitchen. She turned her gaze upon the room and took in the filthy floor, sticky cupboards marked with long drips and grimy patches where dirty fingers regularly pulled at doors and drawers; she surveyed the stained work surfaces, and the teetering pile of crusty dishes by the sink. It was disgusting. "Oh," Frank reappeared in the doorway her for a moment, "I think there's a pair of rubber gloves under the sink if it helps." He smiled, and left her alone.

Ella cleaned. She kept cleaning until everything was as clean as it was ever going to get in that kitchen. From time to time, Frank would appear with some trite encouragement, and then he'd steal a kiss, and disappear again. An hour and a half later, his kisses no longer had their desired effect upon her. Ella took her rubber gloves off and put them back under the sink.

"I'm all done," she called from the hallway.

"Okay," came a mumble from the living room, amidst the sound of onscreen shooting. Then Frank dashed into the hallway, stumbling over the recycling in his hurry.

"You're leaving?"

"Well, yes. I am, after all, finished."

"Oh, well... I'm sorry it wasn't quite what we'd hoped."

"It really wasn't."

"Tell you what, though, why don't we fix for me to come to yours as a cleaner? Coz you don't have any housemates, do you?"

"My place is clean already."

"Well, obviously I wouldn't need to actually do any cleaning, I mean, with no housemates, we could just... you know," he raised his eyebrows fast, twice, and finished the move with a wink.

Ella's mind raced. Should she have him back?

"Okay," she said.

"Of course, I don't actually know your address yet," Frank said.

"I'll text it to you," she said, pulling open the door.

"Hold on," Frank stopped the door with a hand over hers. "Before you do that," he leaned down and closed in on her face, kissing her so gently that she felt it with a twist of longing that seemed to shoot through her whole body. His face lingered, he kissed again. He was so good looking! A shout from the lounge broke the moment, and he pulled away.

Out on the step, she turned to go, but he called her back.

"Here," he said, holding out a five pound note. "You earned this." He grinned.

"I can't take that," she said. "I don't want to take that. I don't want you to pay me."

"I have to pay you, come on, take it!" he waved it at her then lowered his voice. "Someone might be watching, so please, please, take it."

She took it. "I'll put it in a charity box," she said.

"How you spend your earnings is your affair," he laughed at his joke. She walked away, feeling him watching her from behind, but by the time she'd walked the fifty yards to her car, he'd gone back inside.

When Frank rang the doorbell the following week, it wasn't Ella who answered.

"Have I got the right address?" he asked the heavy-set woman in her late sixties, standing in the doorway. Frank pulled his phone from his pocket to check Ella's text. "Fifty-two Minster Street?" he said.

"That's right," the woman replied, arms folded. She studied Frank with one eyebrow raised and the faintest glimmer of a smile on her face. She said nothing more, but let Frank wonder and worry for a few seconds. She didn't look surprised to see him.

Frank checked his phone again. The message with the address had been followed by one with instructions which he'd not read properly. He read it now.

"Oh, I see, there's a sort of password-code thing. Right." He straightened up, waggled his eyebrows and said, "As per instructions, I've come to clean." He finished the sentence with a wink. "Ella sent me."

"Wonderful," the woman replied. "In you come, then. I'm glad of the help because my arthritis has been dreadful lately and it's making it really tricky to get round the backs of the toilet and into all the corners with the duster. And, of course, it's all much worse than usual since we had the puppies. Oh, the mess they make!"

Frank laughed, confused. The woman turned and looked at him, frowning. "Well, come in, then."

"But –"

"That's alright, I've got rubber gloves and everything. And none of us here has got the lurgy, anyway." She moved back into the hall and swept a hand to draw him into the house. "The puppies are all in the garden. Mind you, I don't know what's worse, them or my boys. Three sons I've got, all about your age. I'd have thought they'd have left home by now, but no, they're all still here and as messy as ever. I barely get a moment to myself. It's a great relief to have you come today, and so kind of Ella. And absolutely wonderful of you to do it for just five pounds. Ella gave me the money to pass on to you. So kind, so kind."

Frank stood in the hall, while the woman handed him rubber gloves and a feather duster. He couldn't work out the smile on her face: was she laughing at him?

"Best to start with the dusting," she said, "Start at the top and work your way down, that's the way to clean properly." She handed him an aerosol can of polish spray.

"Is Ella, um, is she, well, does she *live* here?" Frank still failed to grasp the situation.

"Oh no, love, no, no, no. She lives miles away. Miles and miles. Nowhere near here. I know her mother, really, but she doesn't live around here, either. Ella went through primary school with my youngest boy. Lovely girl. One in a million. It'll be a lucky lad who ends up with Ella."

Frank stood, staring, open-mouthed.

A young man appeared from the front room doorway. He was a vast, meaty, solid built chap and he looked like he was in a bad mood. "You can start in my room," he said, arms folded, one eyebrow raised as he took in Frank. "I'll come and watch you do it."

"Here you are, dear, take the polish. Don't forget the duster," the woman smiled and nodded towards Frank. "Thanks ever so much. I'll make you a cup of tea in an hour or so, if you'd like. That's if you feel comfortable having one. No offence taken if not."

As Frank climbed the stairs with his heart in his boots, the woman went to the front door. He didn't see her as she gave the thumbs-up sign and a big wink of her own to Ella, who had watched it all from her car, parked across the road.

Ella returned the thumbs-up, and both women chuckled quietly to themselves as she drove away.

ALONE, TOGETHER

IT WAS ONLY WHEN he played the piano that Julius Wickwire felt truly happy. From the instant his slender fingers connected with the keys on the baby- grand that he'd had to have windows removed in order to install in his lounge, something clicked within him. Some hidden lock was undone and, in that moment, he forgot the complaints of his ex-wife, the lack of contact from his daughter, the wallpaper peeling in his bedroom due to come mysterious source of dampness that no one had been able to identify, the job in accounting that depressed him and, worst of all at this time, his awful new neighbour, Christine Vonnegut.

Christine had moved in just a week before the government had announced the beginning of the lockdown. For the last three weeks, Julius had glimpsed her in the back garden as he worked from the desk that used to be his daughter's. He sat in the pale pink bedroom, posters of One Direction and other popstars he didn't know staring down at him. He watched Christine peg out washing. She was stacking empty cardboard boxes in her shed, presumably as she unpacked them in the house.

Once, Julius had taken a cup of tea into the garden. The weather had turned warm from the moment they'd all been told to stay inside. Of course, on the day when he'd hoped to get a bit of gardening done – on the weekend – it had poured with rain, then snowed and hailed. Typical! But he'd taken his tea out last week, only to have his quiet break interrupted by a voice the other side of the fence.

"Hello? Is somebody there?" it had called.

He had frozen, his lips on the rim of his mug.

"Hello?" the voice came again. "I'm Christine Vonnegut. Your new neighbour. I moved in next door just before the lockdown."

He stood there, lips still poised, still not drinking.

"Hello?"

She doesn't give up easily, he thought.

"I don't like to knock, what with things the way they are, but I wanted to introduce myself."

Still, Julius remained silent and still. He felt as if he were the winner at a game of musical statues.

Eventually, Christine had given up and gone into her house. Julius listened to her footsteps and then heard the back door open and shut. Well aware that she could go upstairs and look out of her back bedroom window and see him standing there like a fool, he threw his cup back and swallowed the tea in a rush that made him cough, then got himself back into his own house, taking care to close his back door quietly, holding the handle so that the lock didn't make a click sound.

And this was the moment the trumpet began blasting out. At first it was just random notes, which Julius realised must be a process of tuning the instrument. Then the scales began: Dear *God*, the scales! Up and down they went, with the occasional jarring blunder. Once she'd done her scales, she began on the arpeggios. This was torture.

Julius didn't have any earplugs. He found some cotton wool in the upstairs bathroom and tore some off, twisted it tightly and rammed it deep into his ears: it didn't work at all.

He put his radio on, loud – but the voices irritated him as much as Christine's trumpet, and, anyway, he could still hear her over them.

He put the television on and turned the volume up. He harrumphed himself down on the armchair, crossed his legs and folded his arms and gritted his teeth until his jaw ached. The programmes were awful and, anyway, they never blotted out the penetrating sound of that blasted horn.

It was while he was pouring himself a little late afternoon sherry that the obvious answer hit him: it was time to fight fire with fire.

Suddenly he found himself *willing* Christine to play. He didn't have to wait long. At around four o'clock, the toot and blast of her trumpet sounded up again. Julius put down his book and headed straight to his baby grand. He settled himself on the stool and imagined himself about to give a concert at the Albert Hall. He even acted out flipping the tails of his jacket behind him as he sat. He rifled through some sheet music, and made his selection with relish.

Next door, the toot-swagger-toot continued. She was playing Gershwin.

Julius selected a piece by Tchaikovsky and laid the music out across the stand. His eyes scanned the pages before him, each dot an instruction as to where his hands must go, and when, in order to translate this language of spots and lines into a majestic tour de force to rival any volume his neighbour might attempt to produce. The baby-grand would surely beat the horn, hands down.

And so his fingers plunged, like starlings onto a wormy lawn, and began to work the keys. The notes thundered and then tinkled, soothed and then enraged as he deftly interpreted the text before him.

He played for two hours, at the end of which his back heaved, his fingers ached, his arms hurt but his revenge felt sweet. He had heard no trumpet, this afternoon. He had beaten her.

He ran a bath to ease his muscles, then read in bed, unable to keep his mind on the plot of his thriller because he was so full of the glee of his victory.

The next day, the trumpeting began in the mid-morning. Julius couldn't be absolutely sure, but it seemed almost certainly as if it were louder than before.

He put down his coffee and hastened to the baby grand. Today, he chose Beethoven. He drowned her out, no problem. He wondered how long it would be, before she gave up.

And so, Julius' days of isolation began to revolve around Christine's practice timetable. Each hour without her brass blasts simply became an hour to wait.

He began to use the waiting time to go through all his sheet music, selecting the loudest and most impressive and intimidating pieces with which to silence his opponent. In the searching, he came across a pile of the jazz pieces his Mother used to get him to play. The memory of her drew him down into a grief he didn't wish to engage with. He left the pile untouched.

Occasionally, necessity demanded that he walk to the corner shop for bread, milk or cornflakes. He found these times increasingly anxiety-inducing, because he was growing convinced that Christine was watching him leaving the house and then practicing from the moment he was gone until the very second that he returned. One time, upon entering his house, he heard the soft sounds of

Corcovado, and rushed to the living room, dropping his shopping in the hall, not caring if his milk got warm. He began to play Chopin's *Fantaisie-Impromptu* as aggressively as he could, but in his panic he made a mess of it, his time signature all over the place and he hit so many wrong notes that, after a few minutes, he drove both hands down hard onto the keys, his foot on the sustain pedal, holding a horrible sound for three furious seconds, then he slammed the lid shut and stormed out of the room. The trumpet stopped, so perhaps he had proved his point.

Julius began coughing about three weeks into the self-isolation. He must have picked something up on one of those visits to the corner shop.

His eyes hurt, and his head throbbed. His chest began to tighten and, drink as he may, he could not soothe the cough. His energy levels flagged. He took to his bed and lay there, drifting in and out of sleep, feeling as if someone had filled his chest with cement and stretched it out almost beyond its endurance. His temperature rose and all thoughts of the piano vanished as the fear began to take hold. He focused on his breathing, and drifted in and out of sleep, getting regularly woken by his own coughing and the fever.

On the eighth day, he felt as if the fever was finally subsiding. He slept better, but still felt weak. As he lay here, wondering if he was, at last, through the worst of it, he became aware of a faint sound: Christine's trumpet. She was playing softly, and as he lay there, he let the music flow over him. The tune was familiar... one of his Mother's favourites... what was it? What *was* it?

Ne Me Quitte Pas. That was it. It came to him as he drifted into sleep. He rested for several hours, and woke to hear the last gentle notes of the *Lullaby of Birdland*. After that, the trumpet fell silent. Julius was surprised to find himself wishing that it might start again.

The next day, a note dropped through his door.

Groceries for you on the step, Christine x

He opened his front door to see a box containing bread, milk, eggs, cereal, sausages and bananas. He took it into his kitchen, placed it on the table, sat down and wept in a way that he hadn't done since his Mother died. How could he thank Christine?

He scrambled some eggs, sprinkled them with salt and devoured them, followed by a banana and a cup of coffee. Then he went to the baby grand, and began to play from memory a piece that his Mother had always got him to play for her in the evenings: *I Got It Bad (And That Ain't Good)*.

His fingers lingered lightly over the keys, remembering as he played, the patterns of the notes buried deep within his subconscious. He played to the middle of the tune, and then suddenly felt completely wiped out, and stopped.

There were a few moments of silence, and then the trumpet came back with, *Here's That Rainy Day*.

Julius absorbed the sound. Here, indeed, was the rainiest of days. When the trumpet stopped, he realised it was his turn. He played the first verse and chorus of *How About You?* and waited for a response. After a couple of minutes, he heard the opening bars of *Don't Get Around Much Anymore*, which made Julius laugh. The laughing soon turned to coughing, and he knew he must rest again. He played the opening bars of *Fever*, and dragged himself back up to bed.

By lunchtime the next day, Julius was feeling stronger again. He sat and played *I'm Beginning To See The Light*.

When he had finished, he waited for a reply. When *C'est Magnifique* started up, he smiled. He paused before beginning the tune that had been on his mind, then cautiously started to play *What Can I Say After I Say I'm Sorry?*

A silence fell. He waited, fiddled with his music, worried that he wouldn't hear back. Then, at last, slowly, slowly, the trumpet called to him; *It Was Just One Of Those Things...* Relieved, he listened, and then responded with, *I'll Remember April*, but he was taken by surprise when the reply came, *I Get A Kick Out Of You*. The only response he could think of was to play *Tea For Two*. As he reached the chorus, he heard the trumpet joining him, and, together, they played the piece through with an enthusiasm that made Julius tremble with joy. When they'd finished, he went and made a fresh cup of tea, which he took into his garden.

"Hello?" he called nervously to the fence.

"Hello," came the reply. "I'm Christine."

MAKING CONTACT

I WOKE IN THE DARK, pulled rudely from a good dream by the insistent buzzing of my alarm clock. It was 3.30am.

I pushed myself up and out from under the care of the duvet, my heart drumming at a lick from the shock of the alarm and also the knowledge of what I was about to do.

The night before, I had taken time to lay a carefully considered outfit upon the mustard velvet chair that squatted cheerfully next to the heavy dark chest of drawers in my bedroom. Now, I slipped my sleep-steeped pyjamas off and pulled on the soft tracksuit bottoms, stretch-cotton sweatshirt and fleece-lined hoodie.

I brushed my teeth lightly, because my gums are always sensitive first thing. I pulled on a pair of pink socks and went downstairs for a cup of tea and a slice of hot toast, thickly buttered all the way to the edges, with a barely-there scrape of marmalade.

I pulled my fingers through my hair and checked my reflection in the mirror by the front door, then lifted my car keys from their hook as quietly as if there were someone to worry about waking, even though there was no one to wake, and stepped over the threshold into the communal hallway. I took the stairs down the four flights to ground level, so that I didn't disturb any of the neighbours in my block with the discordant, industrial clanging of the lift.

Outside, I crossed the carpark to where my dear old bruised Ford Fiesta sat waiting for me. I climbed down into the sagging driver's seat and sat for a moment, key in the ignition, while I checked that the gear stick was in neutral the way my father had taught me to a decade ago. There wasn't a soul in sight, although several flats had lights on. Insomniacs and babies, I supposed: bunnies in their hutches. I wondered again whether I was doing the right thing, slipping across the dark streets of town like a guilty fox.

Nevertheless, I turned the key, reversed out of the space and drove out of the car park, and pulled onto the empty main road.

The sky had changed from black to deepest blue. It was past 4am now, and I was surprised at the number of lights on in the houses I passed. Did this happen every day, I wondered as I waited at the traffic lights on the empty junction, or was everybody's body clock off by now? I drove past the station and the small parade of shops, then through a densely packed residential area and a school, turning left at a large roundabout. At this point in the journey, the buildings fell away and the road pulled me like a thread through the middle of the vast blanket of the common.

The blue sky was brightening tenderly and I could see tall tufty grass clumps across the ground either side of the road. It looked abandoned somehow, and I felt, not for the first time lately, as if I were the only person on the planet, and I had dreamed everything that came before; that this new normal had maybe always been, and it was only now that I was awake to it.

I was nearing my destination. Would they be there? And, again, was I right to be donig this? My doubts told me that I was, probably, wrong to be doing this. But then the yearning kicked in, and the yearning kept my foot on the pedal and the yearning drove me on.

Through the common I wove, praying that the old car wouldn't choose now to have one of its breakdowns. After some minutes more, the heath land became trees, a few at first and then enough to call them woods. The light of dawn kissed the sky and made it blush. I wound my window down a little and felt the air like breath upon my cheek, and I sighed and realised again how quiet I had grown these last few weeks.

A silver-grey star stuck to a tree trunk reflected in my headlights. Just beyond it, as promised, I saw the dark gap between trees which signified that I had arrived at the agreed upon place. I counted twelve other cars parked on the cleared ground, but there were no people in sight. All the cars were small, and my Fiesta looked very much at home as I pulled in between a Fiat and an old Mini Metro.

I turned off the engine and reached for the door handle. Outside, the air was cold and the birds sang the day in with their singular certainty. Once again, the question arose: should I be doing this? My heart was thumping rapidly, pumping fear around my body in a thrilling race.

I decided that, rather than walk straight in, I'd steal silently through the woods, coming from a different angle and remaining hidden so that I could observe it all from a safe distance before making my mind up.

I picked my way between trunks and overhanging branches. After a few minutes, I heard faint voices along with the birdsong. I followed the sounds until I saw them, and when I saw them, I hung back in the deep shade of a horse chestnut, my eyes fixed upon the figures before me.

They were standing in a circle in a small clearing. Already they were less than two metres away from each other. I couldn't see their expressions clearly, but I sensed in each person the same yearning I felt; a keenness to connect.

I'd been invited by an acquaintance who'd emailed me in strictest confidence less than 24 hours ago.

Are you in need of human contact? The message had read. *No words. No I.D. No sexual agenda. We embrace at dawn.*

I watched them now, from the safety of the tree's cover. They hadn't seen me, but were all fixated intensely upon one another. They had arranged themselves into two rows, as if waiting to dance. They stared into each other's faces. Then they reached either side of them and held the hands of the people they stood next to. No one had gloves on. Some were smiling, others seemed to be crying, some giggled and squirmed at the sensation of skin to skin contact after so long.

I thought about stepping out from behind the tree. It hit me hard now, how much I longed to make eye contact with a stranger. How ardently I longed to hold hands with somebody else, anybody else. I realised I had clasped my own hands together in a futile echo of desire.

And then they stepped forward, closer, closer, until they were touching. Arms wrapped around shoulders and torsos, and the people held each other and laughed with wild joy at this act of dangerous rebellion.

I could resist it no more. I stepped out from behind the tree and was about to run towards them when a glaring light came on, causing them all to pull apart, flinching and covering their eyes.

"This is the police," a voice came from somewhere through a megaphone. "We have you surrounded. Please remain where you are. This is an illegal gathering. You're all under arrest."

I watched, frozen to the spot, as the police rushed in and took hold of the huggers. And then, before my eyes, the huggers grabbed hold of them back and began to squeeze them and even wrestle with them, eyeball to eyeball. And the police were shouting, but they were also laughing. And the huggers were whooping with joy at all the riotous, glorious, ungovernable physical contact going on. And I burned with envy at the sight.

The next seconds were all confusion.

Some of the group broke away from the police and fled into the woods in different directions.

I turned and ran back the way I had come. I stumbled over tree roots. Thin branches whipped and slapped against my face and body. Behind me, dogs barked and unseen people shouted.

Thank God, I made it to my car and jabbed the key at the lock, missing and scratching and missing again before catching the lock right and inserting and turning the key, and yanking the door open, banging my head on the frame in my rush to get in. I pulled out of the car park, wheels spinning, seatbelt undone, before anybody else emerged from the woods.

Back on the road, I exhaled with trembling breath. My heart was banging in my chest now and I pulled the seatbelt around me with jerky, shaking tugs. I was sweating hot and cold all at once and struggling to steady my hands on the wheel and drive in a straight line.

A couple of hundred yards along, while my breath was still coming in short puffs, a human form sprang out of the woods to my right, and ran across the road in front of me. I slammed my foot on the brake and pulled an emergency stop.

I sat, wide-eyed and panting, and realised it was a police woman, and that she was pulling one of the escaped huggers from the ditch where the woman must have been hiding. She pulled the hugger's hands behind her back and clipped handcuffs onto them. And all the time she stared at me as if in challenge, daring me to… to what? She could not have seen me hiding behind the horse chestnut, I reasoned, although perhaps she had seen my car parked in the woods…

I held her stare, soaking up the brazen eye contact, willing it to go on and on. I watched the way she took hold of the captured woman's arm with firmness and authority, and guided her back along the road, shooting a final glare through my windscreen as she led her prisoner to where a police car had pulled up and was waiting.

For a moment, I gripped the top of my own left arm with my right hand. I closed my eyes and imagined they were someone else's fingers clasped around my flesh, but I couldn't hurt myself any more than I could tickle myself. I smashed my open palms against the steering wheel and wished with every desperate cell in my body that I had joined them in the clearing.

The last gold of dawn was fading now, giving way to another cloudless day. I drove on, down the long empty road, through the empty common, past the empty school and the shops that were closed, past the homes that were shut up with all those people shut in, and I went back to my silent flat to wait for this to be over.

THE QUIET DAY

A SHORT SECTION of curtain hooks got snapped somehow, I guess from people pulling hard at an angle, leaning over the back of the sofa to pull the curtains together. They caused the top of the fabric to hang down, leaving a drooping yawn in the line. It irritated me now. It hadn't happened all at once, I was sure. They'd snapped one by one, unnoticed. And now, the whole middle section of the left-hand curtain gaped. I was spending so much time in the lounge during lockdown and I felt the absence of the hooks, even when I was engrossed in a box set.

Life had, by now, become a montage of scenes: getting up, making tea, eating badly, watching TV and going back to bed. One had the sense that this was the period that we would emerge from in some kind of altered state, but that no film maker in their right mind would waste any dialogue on it. A fitting piece of background music and a few repetitive clips of action told the audience all that they needed to know. In the same way that Sonny and Cher told Bill Murray it was still Groundhog Day when he woke every morning, we were hanging on in there until the radio played a different tune.

One had time to focus on certain things, like the way that sometimes when you raise a glass of water to your lips, the smell reminds you of the fish tank you had in your bedroom as a child. How the gravel in the bottom would slowly turn a vivid green and how shocking it was to watch a goldfish swim aimlessly with a silly-string of creamy-grey faeces hanging from its body like those old fashioned aeroplanes with banner adverts trailing behind them.

One had time to focus on the people one lived with, too. Constantly. The tics that were forgivable in small doses, when seen for days and weeks on end seemed to grow and dominate and fuel petty resentments that simmered gently yet certainly. I kept a lid on it all, but it was there, bubbling away.

About the third week, a feeling of deep discontentment set in. I sensed that I was not doing this well. The quiet day had finally come and it had caught me unprepared. I yearned to wind back the clock to the announcement of lockdown and start afresh, to do it properly from day one. I would be playing the guitar by now, and working on a novel, and baking with my children. Instead, I had frittered the minutes, hours, days and weeks. Almost a month had passed and I hadn't sorted so much as a sock drawer. I had simply loaded and unloaded the dishwasher, and drunk tea on an endless loop, and checked Facebook and tried to shop online and meanwhile my chance to rectify everything had passed me by. There was no point starting now. Lockdown was sure to be lifted any day. I may as well just wait it out.

By this point, all of us knew someone who'd had it. And we all knew of someone who'd died – a friend of a friend, a friend's relative, in some cases, our own friends and relatives. It was no longer possible to be blasé, to say it was just like flu, to restrict it to a certain type of person. The fear spread, and paranoia took hold.

People stopped posting on Facebook. There was nothing to say, by now. And if you were having a great time, I certainly didn't want to hear about it.

I began to wake in the night, convinced I was getting a temperature, clearing my throat so often that I wasn't sure whether I had a dry cough or not.

When my bread was running low, I would head to the supermarket, all bravado. Then, upon arriving and seeing others in masks, I would take a deep breath while still in my car, and then see how far I could get around the store on one lung's worth. I imagined myself a pearl diver, making a game of it to ease the terror that I felt. Back in the car with my bread, I would slather my hands with viscous alcohol gel that stung in the places where repeated washing had dried my skin. I would pour more out and rub it on my face, where it stung like dry fire.

Having nagged my teenagers about lying in bed til noon, I began to see no point in rising before nine myself. And, even then, what was the point of getting dressed, really?

I could lose any of this at any moment, so what did it matter if my sock drawer was tidy, or my kitchen cupboards well ordered? Who cared if my windows gleamed and my garden was attractive enough to post and share? Why bother planning menus when food was merely fuel and a packet of Pringles could fill you up while you watched TV just as well as a chickpea pilaff and raspberry tart.

What was the point in all the years at work, if I could be laid off at the drop of a hat?

I began to wonder what those long dead and gone would have done with this situation. Not those I had known, like my father, mother and three sisters: I knew what each of them would have done. They would have been sad like I was, and then they would have made tea, stayed indoors and watched television, like I did. Instead, I found myself desperately wondering what Clive James or Victoria Wood would have written, or what Princess Diana or Mother Theresa would have done. What would Anita Roddick's response have been? Gandhi? Churchill? Michael Jackson? Amy Winehouse? Each of them had had the same 24 hours of daytime that I had, but had spent it in such a way that they'd changed the world, rather than watched it pass by their window. What would they do with this time, now? What was the secret they knew, that I had missed?

Increasingly, I forgot to reply to text messages, and eventually I stopped checking my phone altogether. The little machine that had once seemed so important to me responded to this lack of attention by pinging less and less until, one day, it struck me that I hadn't heard from anyone in a whole week.

The hours rolled on with surprising speed. No sooner was I getting up for that first emptying of the bladder than it was time to pee one last time before turning the light out to sleep. I didn't read any more than usual: somehow there didn't seem enough time.

From the windows of my bedroom at the back of the house, I watched a neighbour's newly landscaped garden. They had planted four fruit trees along the line of their fence and, despite their twig-slender appearance, blossom was now flowering on each skinny branch. But the earth which had been cleared beneath them was now hidden beneath a solid covering of weeds. I watched them spreading, thicker every day. My neighbour had cleared this patch of land several times over the last year in preparation for the fruit trees. Now they were in. I understood his loss of heart in doing anything about the weeds, but it was depressing to see his efforts thwarted by nature. It took me two more weeks to realise that he should have taken hold of the soil while it was pure, lying there rich and fertile and empty, and planted some grass seeds. At least then the weeds couldn't have won, and when his fruit matured, he could enjoy the feeling of young, bright grass beneath bare toes as he tasted his first home-grown apple.

As the sixth week drifted into view, I found myself lost in a deep, dark sea, tossed and sucked down by waves of reflection and regret. I felt as if I faced a tsunami on a paddleboard. Childhood memories flooded over me, and with them came the horrors of hindsight, the recollections of conversations with parents and teachers who'd offered guidance which I'd ignored. The pain of regret engulfed me, and I went to the shed at the bottom of the garden, closed the door and howled like an animal with an open wound.

Like a jigsaw forming itself before my mind's eye, I saw how all those choices I'd made had built and connected and formed the fabric of my life as it was now. I saw both the roots of my arrogance and the fruits. I saw every effect of my apathy, my short term vision, my lack of ambition, my failure to persevere until a goal was reached. I saw the times I'd said no when I should have said yes, and the times I'd said yes when I should have said no.

I saw the paths I had taken and, with an empty, hollow feeling, saw that they had led me away from opportunities. I saw that each path I'd taken had taken me in a sort of spiral walk so that my world had become smaller and smaller. I had closed things down at every opportunity to open them up. I had shrunk the world to a safe size, only to discover that there was nothing safe about the place I now found myself in.

Life began to feel like an insurmountable catalogue of failures: friendships that I'd left to drift until I'd lost touch with many good people; countries I'd never been to; languages and instruments I'd never learned.

It became too much. Television offered no escape and I couldn't concentrate on books.

For three days, I only left my bedroom to go to the toilet or get water. I lay on my back, often with the covers over my face, and despaired.

On the second day, the kids pushed my bedroom door open and peered into the curtained gloom.

"I'm alright," I said. "Leave me be. I just need to rest."

Still, they lingered.

"Why don't you go on YouTube and try to learn Italian or something," I said. "Make the most of your spongey young brains."

That got rid of them, and I realised with a physical sensation that made me wince that they wouldn't take any advice from me, either. They would make all their own mistakes, a whole new list of errors. What was the point of life when hindsight was the only marker? I felt I couldn't bear to continue in the face of my regret and sadness.

We had been stripped back and stripped bare, and all I could feel was, what was the point in even trying when it could all be taken away from you at any moment?

And with this thought in my head, I closed my eyes and slept, for eighteen hours straight.

I was woken by my daughters. They were sitting on my bed, the pair of them studying my face. They looked serious as their faces came slowly into focus.

"Are you alright, Dad?" Jess, my eldest, asked.

"Do you need us to call anyone?" My youngest, Beth, stroked the duvet.

I closed my eyes.

"Dad, don't go back to sleep. Please!" Jess said.

But I didn't seem able to open my eyes.

"I'm sorry," I managed, but I couldn't say anymore. A tear rolled down the side of my head and soaked into the pillow.

"Dad," the girls pressed, but I turned my face away.

I'm sorry," I repeated. Eventually they left the room.

I was lost, completely. And I was trapped. I couldn't leave my girls to cope alone. In that time, terrible thoughts crossed my mind. The girls returned, but I remained with my eyes closed until they left me alone.

And then I smelt burning.

It was a faint suspicion at first, but there was no denying it: something was on fire.

Suddenly I was moving. Out of bed, out of the bedroom, down the stairs and to the lounge, then the kitchen: I couldn't find any fire. The back door was open, and I stepped into the garden.

Jess and Beth were sitting by the barbeque, which they had lit. They had marshmallows on forks that they were toasting over the flames. They looked up at me and smiled, but there was anxiety in both their faces.

"How are you?" Jess asked.

"Hungry," I said.

They both held their marshmallows up to me. I ate them both with a gratitude that set me weeping. The girls came and threw their arms around me, and we sat and cried together.

"We've been so worried, Dad," they said, their tears running onto my T-Shirt.

"I'm sorry," was all I could manage, but a thought flashed through my mind. This could all be taken away from me at any moment. The marshmallow was burnt and fixed itself to my teeth and the girls laughed as I protested its super-glue stickiness.

That evening, I took the bag of curtain hooks from the sewing basket, and fixed the gaping curtain, threading each hook through the double loops of stitching on the back of the fabric, and then pushing the tapered end of the hook through the plastic loop that hung from the curtain rail. O my astonishment, it took only four hooks to close the hole up.

I stepped down off the stool and admired my work. Tomorrow, maybe I'd see if the girls wanted to go for a walk.

Old Maid's Field

WE ONLY MANAGED to get our teenage daughter out for one walk during the entire lockdown period. It was actually on a cooler day, which seemed a shame after all the glorious sunshine we'd had. We went to a rough, wild orchard called Old Maid's Field, in a valley that had once belonged to a wealthy spinster who bequeathed the land to the community upon her death.

By this time, Nina had been in her room for a solid six weeks. I knew she was eating, because dirty plates appeared in the sink, and the kitchen cupboards depleted steadily in their stocks of noodles and peanut butter. I knew she was watching Netflix on her computer, because often when I tried to watch a film, the television informed me that it was not possible for me to do so due to Nina's using it up above me.

As a small child, Nina couldn't keep away from me. How I had longed for some space between us, back then! Hard to imagine that, now. She used to wrap her arms around my legs and cling on tight. It drove me crazy. I used to have to let her accompany me to the bathroom. I remember how I yearned for the day when I could sit on a toilet and not answer questions about exactly what I was doing at each stage of the process.

She would come with me everywhere, and howl at leaving me. People said she had separation anxiety. Now, I think perhaps I'm the one with separation anxiety. I miss her, terribly, in ways I could never have imagined or believed back then. It actually *hurts*. Every time I go to the loo I picture her little self beside me and something somewhere deep inside me aches a little, like a fairy, groaning.

I am surprised to find that I miss baking and painting and junk modelling and reading and gardening together... all those little things that felt like a torturous waste of life, a way of merely killing time until bath-time and bed-time: oh, how I miss bath-time and bed-time! And, as I say that, I wonder *how* I *can* miss bath and bed-time, as they drove me insane with their repetitive tedium.

Every night she'd have us make up a song to get her to sleep. She'd say, "Make it a song about a ladybird and a sunflower," or "Make it a song about a fairy and a pig." I used to think my head would fall off with the round and round of it all.

And then, at some point, somewhere around thirteen or fourteen, she disappeared. I don't mean she ran away. She was physically present, but... somehow also not there at all. She was cut off from me, as if there were a sheet of glass between her and the world I lived in. Messages and conversations with her friends became private, secretive transactions. It was as if she worked for MI5. Intruding upon her meant receiving a look that could, just maybe, actually *kill* you.

But, underneath all the make-up and fashion experiments (she's stealing make-up from me and clothes from her father's drawers these days, and going about wearing them as if we're a couple of morons who don't realise), I cling on to the fact that, really, no one knows my daughter better than I do. I mean, she was *so* dependent upon me. I was her *world*, and she mine. There's not a hair on her head that I haven't checked for lice and fought with a comb; not a freckle on her body that I haven't seen and memorised; not a thought in her mind that could possibly surprise me. I *know* her, inside out.

She is sweet and shy, and wouldn't hurt a fly. She likes unicorns and cupcakes and wings that you can wear with your arms through the straps. She loves waving wands and making wishes. I know the *essence* of Nina. I could make a perfume of her, I know her that well, and it would smell of candyfloss and strawberries.

When she emerged from her room today, like a moth from a cocoon, I was stunned to hear her request to go for a walk. I didn't question it, though. I grabbed this opportunity to reconnect, and we set off to Old Maid's Field.

She didn't speak in the car all the way there. She put her headphones in and stared out of the window. I put Radio 4 on, and acted like I didn't mind. I parked in the residential street by the lane that led down through the woods to Old Maid's Field. We got out of the car, put on coats, (although it was sunny, there was an unkind wind), and I locked the car by pointing the key fob at it over my shoulder, and pressing a button as I crossed the road.

We walked down the muddy pathway still boggy from recent rain. I thought about how I hate the countryside because mud looks just like poo to me and walking on it makes me feel horribly dirty. I never brought Nina to places like this when she was little. Play parks were about as close to nature as we ventured. And the beach, on holiday.

She still hadn't spoken a word to me – and I hadn't to her, either. We lolloped down the hill; lollopy, lollopy, lollopy, getting dirtier with every step. I resisted the urge to recite nursery rhymes about farmers and tractors and hobbledy-hoy. I've done that before and I don't wish to receive the withering look such reminiscence invites.

At one moment, a single headphone still jammed into one ear while the other dangled down, she turned to me and smiled. It lifted my spirit more than I would have thought possible. It was like one minute I'd been alone, and the next, I'd felt in the best company imaginable. And then she looked away, ahead, and I was alone again. The sun seemed to go in. The woods felt cold and uncertain.

Just when I felt I'd had as much woods as I could bear, we stepped out of the brown and into the bright blue, green and white of an apple orchard. It was as if someone had taken the lid off and let the light in. The trees were old and gnarled, their twisted branches bent and knobbly as arthritic fingers. I wished Nina were little so that I could take her in my arms and hold her up to inhale the full, perfumed clumps of pinky-white blossom. But she was tall enough to reach to breathe it in without any help from me; indeed, she was taller than me now. When I suggested she sniff it, she chose not to.

She wandered off without me, not waiting to check whether I was following or not. Of course, I followed, just in case she should say something, make some charming observation or recall a beautiful memory. Or she might need me. There were stinging nettles about. I had a tube of bite cream in my bag, just in case, and some antiseptic and two sticking plasters.

She pushed on, through the long grass, not waiting to reminisce about that Bear Hunt book that she used to love so much. There were no outwards signs that she was even thinking of it like I was.

Suddenly, without warning, she began to run about the orchard, weaving between trees. Her long hair bounced out behind her. She was so graceful, the sight of her stopped me in my tracks. I stood and watched her. She was strong and sure of her movements. She'd gone a good couple of hundred yards from me now, and she stopped running just as suddenly as she had started. She turned and looked straight at me, right into my eyes from all that way off. My heart lifted in recognition of her need.

"I'm here!" I called, far more cheerfully than was necessary, as if I was lucky.

But she didn't answer. Instead, she began wandering about, weaving and looping between the trees. When she thought I wasn't looking, I saw her sniff the apple blossom, which also made me glad, in a sad sort of way.

There was one tree which had fallen, struck by lightning at some point with a hit that had split its trunk in two. I perched uncomfortably upon its old weathered bark now, and took out the Twix I had grabbed before leaving home. Nina wandered and wound in and out of the trees. She looked like an artist's muse, bohemian and wild. There was something of the Emily Brontë about her, I thought.

She wasn't interested in me, so I decided to act in similarly oblivious fashion. I tried to concentrate on the trees and the sky and the Twix, without looking at her at all. No sooner had I made the decision to ignore her than she plonked her weight down upon the tree branch, next to me. I couldn't hide the pleasure I felt, like a cat who's been stroked by a passer-by and purrs with cheap gratitude. I reached into my bag and gave her the other Twix. We ate in silence.

Then she said, as casually as if she were commenting on the fair weather or the green grass, "I wish I was a Victorian ghost. I'd like to haunt a place like this. To follow people between trees, to be glimpsed from a distance, to be sepia-coloured…"

"Really?" I tried to pair this information up with the Nina I knew, the Nina of rainbows and cupcakes. I tried to match it up like socks from the wash but it would not correspond. "*Really?*"

She was up and wandering again, not interested in my confusion. She left half her Twix on the tree stump. I ate it as I watched her explore without me. I didn't like how far she was going. I felt suddenly alone, exposed and vulnerable, sitting here like this in the middle of some lonely old woman's waste ground.

"Nina!" I called. She looked around. "Nina! Wait for me!" I stuffed the Twix wrappers into my pocket and ran in an effort to catch up with her.

Learning Journal for Gloria Madeleine Hooper 30ᵀᴴ April 2020

TASK: Encourage your child to make a list of all the things they learned after a day of home schooling. They should write this, double spaced with a finger space between each word, in their Topic Book for their teacher to enjoy when they return to school.

I Am Gloria Madeleine Hooper and these are all the things I learned today.

1. Orange juice instead of milk on Coco Pops is disgusting.

2. Wasting food makes Daddy shout.

3. Spilling juice hits all of Mummy's buttons because it costs a lot of money and Daddy's job is gone and now it's all down to Mummy and she doesn't earn as much as Daddy even though she went to two universities and he only went to one.

4. It's just as important for adults to say sorry as for children and we must try not to shout at each other but that is hard because we're living together all the time and we're only human.

5. We are religious. I know this because I hear Mummy thanking God all day long for CBeebies.

6. Daddy hated maths at school so, so much, probably even more than I do and he has no idea what bus stops have to do with sums.

7. I can eat seven biscuits before getting caught.

8. 40 at 40 is the only setting I will ever need to learn on any washing machine I ever have in my whole entire life.

9. Chocolate tastes best when it's been dipped in Mummy's tea.

10. It's best not to tell Mummy if you're doing that because she doesn't like her tea being messed with.

11. If you don't eat your lunch but you did eat a whole entire chocolate egg left from Easter, plus eleven biscuits, everyone gets cross.

12. My fingers can touch each other now when I wrap them around Mummy's middle.

13. Daddy likes to read books called thrillers. I listened while he read one to me, but I didn't learn anything doing that.

14. After three pages, Daddy falls asleep.

15. Mummy still has to do everything, even though we are all at home now.

16. Mummy used to have a boyfriend when she was at school, and his name was Jake Gardener, and he was absolutely gorgeous like a model.

17. All the girls loved Jake, but Jake only liked my Mummy.

18. Mummy told Jake she wouldn't be his girlfriend anymore when she met Daddy, because Daddy's jokes were funnier than Jake's.

19. Jake is now living at the top of a tree in a bank and he has money coming out of his ears because Mummy Googled him last week.

20. Daddy's jokes aren't as funny as they used to be.

21. It is very hard for Mummy to balance. It's hard for all women to balance.

22. Most men never have to worry about balancing.

23. I'm ok balancing now, but it will hit me when I'm about twenty-three.

24. Sometimes adults wonder what it is all about.#

25. Daddy's arms can reach around both Mummy and me at the same time.

26. Mummy's tickle-bone is still just as tickly as the day Daddy first tickled her.

27. Actually Daddy can still actually make Mummy laugh actually, even though his jokes are so bad.

28. The biscuit tin can balance on Daddy's tummy.

29. If I press my face into Daddy's tummy, my nose doesn't get squashed, it just goes right on in.

30. It's A Wonderful Life is Mummy *and* Daddy's favourite film, and you can watch it in Spring just as well as you can watch it at Christmas.

31. Mummy and Daddy both love my school, even though Mrs. Caplan is so strict.

32. These days, Mummy and Daddy wish Mrs. Caplan would come to live at our house and do lockdown with us.

33. Mummy and Daddy love me more than anything. Maybe I shouldn't add that to this list, because I already learned that before. But I was happy to learn it again.

One Last Sunset

KIM STOOD AT THE FOOT OF THE STAIRS, staring at the message on the phone in her hand, her eyebrows drawn tightly together. She shook her head.

"How can they expect you to go back to school, now?"

She looked at her daughter, halfway up the staircase, who turned and shrugged in response.

"I don't think I want you to go back," Kim said.

"It'll be nice to see my friends again," Hannah said, picking at her nails.

"You haven't picked at your cuticles for weeks," Kim said.

"And? What do you mean?"

"I mean you're not stressed like you always are at school. Just one mention of going back and you're picking at your nails."

"Well, I've gotta go back at some point, Mum. This time next year I'll be sitting my GCSEs."

"Yes, but why *now*? What's changed at this point?"

"I don't know."

"Stuff it, you're not going back. Neither of us are. Pack a bag."

"Mum, what?" Hannah stared at her mother. "What are you saying?"

"We're off. Chuck your stuff in a bag and let's go."

"What stuff?"

"I don't know! Pj's, toothbrush… trackie bottoms, I suppose."

Hannah held her mother still for a moment with a look. "Mum, where will we go? Just think about this for a moment, ok? Because you realise that Covid is everywhere, right? And the Government –"

"The Government? Ha! Stuff the Government! They're the people who didn't lock us down immediately. They're the ones who let massive sporting fixtures happen when we should have been isolating. They're the ones who said there actually were a different set of rules for Dominic Cummings. They have no idea what to do. They're making it up as they go along. Let's do the same."

"O-kay," Hannah looked uncertain. She came down the stairs and stood next to her mother. "What do you suggest?"

"What do I suggest?" Kim's mouth twitched and then grew into a wide smile. "What do *I* suggest? Hannah, you never used to give a biscuit for what I thought, let alone considering anything I suggested! This is *crazy*!" She saw Hannah's look of alarm and gave her a quick kiss on the cheek. "Crazy in a *good* way!"

"Well, what do you mean?" Hannah ran a hand through her split ends. "Of course I've always listened to what you think and say."

Kim shook her head and marvelled, still smiling at how she could have become such an influence on her daughter: four months ago, Hannah could not look at her without scowling. Now, here they stood, friends in adversity. There was no way Kim was letting this go.

"I'll barricade us in. They'll have to come and get you if they want you," she declared. She ran to the front room and grabbed a handful of pink and green cushions and began piling them against the front door.

"Mum, don't! Stop it!" Hannah began dismantling the pile as quickly as Kim could build it, laughing as she hurled the cushions back onto the sofa.

"Or we could go and live in the middle of nowhere, and I'll home school you."

"Mum, I love you dearly, but we both know that's not a good idea."

"Hannah, I'm serious." Kim grabbed a set of keys from a hook by the door. "Get in the car. Never mind the bags. We'll buy pyjamas wherever we end up."

As they drove out of town, a bag for life in the back seat packed with wash things, pyjamas and a couple of pairs of clean knickers, Hannah began to giggle. Kim frowned. "What?"

"Mum, are we kidnapping each other? Or running away from home together? I mean, what are we actually *doing* here?"

Kim passed a trembling hand quickly over her forehead, caught a stray strand of hair that was tickling her eye and tucked it back behind her ear. "I don't know," she said. "I guess... I guess..." she sighed. "I honestly don't know." She drove without paying attention to left or right, she just drove and drove. "There's our first post box," she brightened at the sight of the red pillar box topped with a crocheted cap with crochet flowers and robins sewn onto it. "Remember that one?"

"The first one we did," Hannah smiled.

"It still looks good. And no one's vandalised it."

"In fact I think people may have added to it," Hannah said. "I'm sure there are more flowers on there than there were when we first put it up. It was great coming up here in the night to put it on the post box, then driving away like criminals. Remember how paranoid we were? And that police car came up behind us and you pulled over, but of course it wasn't chasing us and it just drove on past," Hannah threw her head back and laughed a loud, belly laugh. "You were so scared!"

Kim sniffed and Hannah stopped, turning suddenly to her mother.

"Mum, are you crying?"

Kim sniffed again in reply and slowed down the car a little. "I can't help myself. It's too much. Too much staying home, too much risk going out… I mean, what if you go to school, pick up the virus, and then bring it home? What if I get it and then… Well, *you* need me. I'm needed. I can't leave you now. This virus is still as serious as it was on day one."

"Mm." Hannah looked down at her smooth finger-tips, free of all the usual soreness at last. "If you're worried, then I won't go."

The streets were quiet in the late afternoon. Kim pulled the car smoothly around a bend, past quiet houses. Everything felt so tidy and contained.

"It's just that this time together has been getting better and better. I love waking up and pottering about. And, anyway, look at *this*! This would normally be rush hour, but here we are, driving without stopping. I can crawl along at my usual speed and no one honks their horn at me!"

"Yeah, but where are we actually *going*, Mum?"

Kim turned the radio on and ignored the question. Hannah sighed and watched her world go by through the car window. A thought struck her as they passed an office block.

"Won't your work go back soon, anyway?"

"I suppose so, but... Oh, Hannah! How can we escape all -" she flapped her hand at the window with a gesture like an inept version of the royal wave, "- this?"

"Mum, I know you don't want to hear this, but..." She sighed. "I've been teaching myself maths since March and I have no idea if I'm right or wrong on any of it. I *need* other people."

Kim shook her head. "Well, I'm not sure I *do*. It's scary out there right now. And I don't want to go back to visiting my miserable father out of guilt, or going to parties that scare me out of duty, or driving across the country to weddings of people I'll never see again. The last four months have shown me the people I want to be in touch with. There are five of them, and you're one. I don't want the rest of it."

Hannah reached out and took her mother's hand. "Mum, I get it. But... I miss my friends."

"I know you do. I know." Kim looked over at her daughter, who had grown several inches taller during lockdown. "I suppose the idea of sending you back feels a lot like your first day at school, all over again. I was used to you being more independent of me, and now – well, I've loved being with you and getting to know you all over again. And there's still so many jobs I haven't done. I don't want to let go of this time. I don't want to get back on the treadmill. But I know it'll happen, because it just *does*. This time next year, we'll all be stressed off our heads again with to-do lists longer than our arms...
And you won't want to speak to me or tell me anything and I will be back to having no idea what goes on in your day or in your head."

Hannah inhaled deeply, held the breath and then pushed it out. "Take a right, here," she said.

"Right? What, here?" Kim clicked the indicator up.

"Yes."

"Where are we going, Hannah?"

"Let's go down to the sea," Hannah said.

Kim nodded.

They drove on, in comfortable, purposeful silence, down to the seafront. Kim parked on the esplanade where they had sat together for so many evenings these last few months. They scrabbled through the glove box until they found the packet of Polos there, and they watched the sun make its slow descent over the sea. It seemed hardly to move for a long time, and then suddenly, it was gone.

As the sky darkened, Hannah turned to her mother. "Let's go home," she said. Like an obedient child, Kim nodded and accepted her instructions. "Alright," she said meekly, turning the key in the ignition.

Driving slowly home, they passed another of their post-boxes with more crocheted birds pecking at flowers on it. Kim found the tears were rolling down her face again as she drove, making it difficult to focus on the road ahead, blurring the green lights that she wished were red.

"There's nothing to stop us coming out at night to crochet-bomb more post boxes," Hannah said. She placed her hand upon her mother's as she changed down a gear on a steep hill. "And there will be another sunset, Mum," she said, "Whatever else happens."

"Whatever else happens," Kim smiled at her daughter, and turned to face the road ahead.

ABOUT THE AUTHOR

Liz Jennings is a writer and writing group facilitator, specialising in designing and running writing groups with and for people with dementia.

Her other books include Blank For Your Own Message, a collection of short stories about parents and children, and Short Christians, a collection of short stories that explore Christian faith experiences through fiction, both published by Lioness. She is the editor of Welcome To Our World, a collection of life writing by people with dementia, which raises funds for the Alzheimer's Society.

Liz hosts two websites: Lizjenningswriter.com, where she blogs and posts writing encouragements and occasional online writing groups, and Lastminutesmallgroup.com, a site full of instant resources for time-poor church small group leaders.

Liz grew up in Streatham, South London, and now lives in Canterbury, Kent.

Blank For Your Own Message is a collection of short stories inspired by the crazy world of parenting young children.

Tales include that of a single father trying to get insurance against being disappointed by his son, a woman who's tempted to steal toys while at a children's birthday party, a childminding grandma who gets stuck between two rollers in a soft play centre, and tea in a supermarket café which ends with a handbag full of vomit.

"As a busy mum who rarely gets time to delve into long novels anymore, I've loved picking this up in between chores and play times! I've laughed, I've cried, I've giggled and gasped (and winced when I've recognised myself)! An enjoyable read for any parent!" – FunMom, Amazon

"A brilliant piece of writing. Engaging and page turning."- Mr.B, Amazon

Short Christians is a collection of twelve engaging stories about realistic, down-to-earth Christian characters dealing with the challenges of everyday life and faith.

Enjoy this book with your small group to spark fresh thinking, discussion and points of connection in an accessible and enjoyable way, or savour it individually, reflecting on your reactions to characters and events to journey deeper into your own faith experience.

Each story is followed by discussion questions, encouragement to listen to what the bible says, points for prayer and space for your own journaling. In addition, this volume includes author notes, revealing intriguing insights into the inspiration behind the stories.

"A great tool for small groups to open up honest discussions that go a little deeper!"- Sarah, Small Group Member

"...a genuinely useful book, both within a group context and as a means for private reflection..." – Waterstones' reader

You can enjoy the power of stories to build bridges and bring people together in your church with a fun, accessible and interactive *Short Christians* session put together by Liz. Groups can be facilitated in person, or electronically if you are running virtual church gatherings.

"It helped me think about how other people in church might be feeling." – Anne, group attendee, Canterbury

"Best breakfast session for some time! You have a wonderful engaging, relaxed, honest style that is perfect for our group. I hope you were blessed as much as you blessed us!" – Helen, church events' organiser, Sidcup

To talk about how your church family could connect and build deeper relationships through the stories of *Short Christians*, contact Liz via Lastminutesmallgroup.com

Printed in Great Britain
by Amazon